He Danced with a Chair

TED WALKER

He Danced
with a Chair

FICTIONS AND FACTIONS

London Magazine Editions

First published in Great Britain 2001
by London Magazine Editions
30 Thurloe Place, London SW7 2HQ
Copyright © 2001 Ted Walker
ISBN 0–904388–88–3
Set in Monotype Ehrhardt by
Rowland Phototypesetting Ltd
Printed in Great Britain by
St Edmundsbury Press Ltd
both of Bury St Edmunds, Suffolk

A CIP catalogue record for this book
is available from the British Library

For old chums –
including one who danced with a chair –
before it's too late.

CONTENTS

ACKNOWLEDGEMENTS

Eight of these stories appeared originally in the *New Yorker* Magazine and four in *Good Housekeeping*. Others appeared originally in *McCall's*, the *Virginia Quarterley*, the *London Magazine*, the *Atlantic Monthly*, the *Boston University Journal* and on BBC Radio 4.

REMEMBERED LETTERS

When I was thirteen, I wrote to the Dalai Lama. I had been ill (more seriously than I knew), and in the weeks while I recovered my strength I read all the books on Tibet my mother could find in the local libraries. It was 'Lost Horizon' that started me off – a paperback edition with a broken spine. The only other title I recall is 'Twenty Years in Tibet.' Once while I was alone in the house, I tried my hand at carving butter. Before anyone came home, I smoothed the butter back into its oblong dish and put it away. A natural linguist (my father had me taught French and German by the Berlitz method), I wondered, and worried, about the correct pro-nunciation of '*Om mani padme hum.*' This was years before mantras were to become everyday in the Western world. In a magazine I found a colour photograph of a lotus flower. I pinned it to my bedroom wall and stared at it, imagining the jewel it contained. My dressing gown (mushroom: the closest I could get to saffron) doubled as a monk's robe. When I was almost better and allowed to get up, I wrote my letter. It was short and reverential, and it contained, between my greeting and homage, a polite request for an English-speaking pen friend. I searched in Pears Cyclopaedia for the correct mode of address for the Dalai Lama. The information was lacking, though I did learn, should I ever need to know, how to address a viscount, a marchioness, or the Archbishop of Armagh. I settled for 'My Lord,' and hoped to be forgiven if I had committed a solecism. The Dalai Lama was, I understood, a boy of my own age. On the envelope, beneath his title, I wrote, 'The Potala Palace, Lhasa, Tibet.' There was consternation at the village post office. Mrs Armitage, the postmistress, didn't know what to charge, Tibet not being listed under international postal tariffs. I asked for stamps appropriate for China, and added three more halfpenny stamps, which, if memory serves, in those days were a pleasant emerald green. 'It will never get there,' Mrs Armitage told me. 'The country's not listed.' But I posted the letter, confident that the extra stamps would generate a sense of urgency and expedition in the mail. Indeed, it was eight and a half months before my letter was returned to me, marked 'Undeliverable.' It had been a particularly severe winter, I concluded, and the Sherpa team had not got through. By now I was fit and well and interested in cricket.

*

At eighteen (cricket having palled), I fell in love and began to write poems. My poems were tactile. My ample girlfriend wore improbably thick coats, but in the local gallery there was a statue one could handle. The girl respected me for my mind, to which verse (not only my own) adhered like summer bugs to a flypaper. She gave me – and for this I forgave her her coats – the 'Collected Poems 1909–35' of T. S. Eliot. At school I had been given the impression that Tennyson had been the last, the very last, of English poets.

I wrote to Mr Eliot, at Faber & Faber, to let him know that I, too, was practising the art. My letter was written in violet ink on magenta paper and was sealed in an envelope of faded burgundy. I wrote to him as an equal, in a copperplate hand I had taught myself from advertisements for Player's No-Name tobacco. The writing made exquisite use of the space available. I put Eliot right on a few points concerning some snatches of French verse he'd filched. All very well, I said, but it should be quoted exactly, if at all. On the other hand, I said, I defended him against my father's criticism that there was no *particular* way in which a madman shook a dead geranium. (Madmen, my father had said, would shake a dead geranium, or dead gerania, in much the same fashion as sane men would. 'You perversely miss the essential point,' I'd told my father.) It was a very long time before I heard from Eliot. He sent my letter back, having made pencil squiggles in my margins. 'Deliberate' and 'Derivative,' he marked against my reference to Laforgue. 'Thank you,' he wrote adjacent to the word 'geranium.' By this time, I had a sense of my own callowness. The copperplate looked as false as it was, and the violet ink made me sorrowful. Eliot had been kind to me. I was grateful to him and scathing of myself. I put the letter between the pages of Volume II of my father's Modern Carpenter, Joiner and Cabinet-maker, where all the important family documents – birth certificates and such – were kept. I think of it whenever Eliot is mentioned. I thought of it the day I stood in his office at Faber & Faber (he'd been dead several years; I never met him), and I wondered if he had stood at the window for a moment trying to decide whether to toss the magenta sheet away or spare me a minute of his life. I could hear the sound of horse's hooves in the streets somewhere outside in Bloomsbury. The

3

day he died – the moment of his death, as I discovered later – I was driving past Pevensey Castle on my way to visit a poet in Rye. That evening, I called in at my father's house and asked to see the letter. It had been lost. We looked in every volume of the encyclopedia, and found a dozen or so photographs and newspaper clippings to remind us of times past. I still have the Collected Poems. I wish I had the letter. I think that every so often, apropos of nothing in particular, I would have thought of it, looked at it, put it away.

*

Gough Island is in the South Atlantic, not quite halfway from the Cape of Good Hope to Cape Horn. It is a British possession. The summer of my graduation from Cambridge, I was invited to join the university scientific survey of the island, which at the time was uninhabited. My task would have been to write the book of the expedition – the human-interest story, that is, not the grim stuff about plants, rocks, creatures and climate. I turned down the offer. I was getting married in the middle of August, and the bridesmaids' dresses were already cut out and tacked. However, I did my bit to help the preparations. For example, I carried quantities of rope from an upper room at the Scott Polar Research Institute down to the street. The rope was loaded into the back of a green 1926 Morris 'bullnose' owned by my friend Roger, the expedition's geologist. (Roger, had he not gone to Gough Island, would have been best man at my wedding.) Home from our honeymoon in the Tyrol, I wrote a letter to Roger, telling him what he had been missing by not staying in England. He'd missed, for example, the film 'Genevieve' and some notable batting performances by Denis Compton in the county cricket championship. The address on the envelope looked stark: after Roger's name I wrote, 'Gough Island, South Atlantic.' On second thought, I added, 'Near Tristan da Cunha.' Needless to say, the letter was never delivered. Nor was it returned to me. I do still have the letter Roger wrote to me, though. The envelope would be of special interest to philatelists, having Tristan da Cunha stamps cancelled with the expedition's own marks. Roger didn't tell me a great deal, apart from the fact that the little party of scientists dined off a wandering albatross on Christmas Day. But when I grow maudlin and loquacious after a few drinks, I have a way of regaling the company with information about Gough Island. I give long, graphic, and detailed descriptions of the rugged terrain, the lofty cliffs, the Hag's Tooth mountain. There are plants that grow there and nowhere else. There are mice – ordinary little house mice – which must have come ashore when Capain Gough made his landfall in the mid-eighteenth century. I can't remember where I learned these facts. I suppose they *are* facts. Oh, and Roger added a P.S. to his letter. When the party was put ashore from the Tristania, the expedition leader collapsed, apparently from a slipped disc, while poking about on the beach. He went straight back to Tristan after the provisions and gear were unloaded, and from Tristan a Royal Navy frigate took him to Cape Town. So it was that neither he nor I wrote the book. Sad.

*

By my mid-twenties, I was the father of three. I was a schoolmaster. We were abjectly poor, and we had expensive tastes. In a room so damp fungi grew along the waist-high

5

tidemark on the walls, my wife and I would sip Armagnac after a meal of turnip-and-potato soup. One summer, I took a vacation job as tour leader for Thomas Cook. The pay was poor, but with the tips I received I was able to bring home duty-free wines, spirits, and cigars each time I crossed the Channel with a group of tourists. We ate meat – sometimes four times a week – from mid-July to the beginning of September. The children thrived. I grew very depressed. It seemed that we should never emerge from our chronic debts. I felt cornered, frantic, as the new school term approached. During the final crossing of the summer, from Dieppe to Newhaven, I sat in the first-class bar, and on the back of a menu I wrote down a full account of my wretchedness. The first half was in French, the second in English. My style was extravagant. I was self-pitying in a manner redolent of, say, the worst of Alfred de Musset. There were twelve lines of classical Alexandrine followed by twelve in iambic pentameter. When I had done, I wrote my name and address at the bottom. The barman gave me an empty Yellow Chartreuse bottle. I rolled up my verse, secured the stopper. I cast it from the quarterdeck in mid-Channel. When I returned to my drink, the barman offered me a piece of advice I have always followed: 'Buy what you want, whatever it is, and haul your salary up behind you.' Gradually, our financial position did improve. The more we spent, the better job I moved to. I got out of teaching, went into broadcasting, publishing, and, finally, the wine trade. Sometimes I wonder if anybody ever found my *cri de coeur*, or whether the bottle slowly filled with water and sank. I've never, myself, found a message in a bottle. But I was with a friend once when he found one. It was in a lemonade bottle, which I thought lacked panache. The message was short and poignant – particularly for me, as it was saying, in its way, what I had said in mine. My friend still has it. It reads: 'I am a young, intelligent, and hardworking man. I have a boring job with no prospects, and I despair of making a success of my life. If anybody should find this and can give me sound advice, please contact me at the address below.' My friend and I sat on a breakwater for a long time trying to decide what to do. It was an embarrassing responsibility. We both knew the young man. He lived in our village, worked in the village shop. Next to his name he'd written the date. He must have cast his bottle on the morning tide the day my friend found it. That was five years ago. The man still works in the village shop; this very morning, he sold me a superb Brie. He seems fretfully happy whenever I see him.

*

When a man enters middle age, he is inclined, for a short while, to become portentous. His children appear to know as much as he knows on certain subjects. He makes out his will, and deposits it in his bank. He may even – as I did a couple of years back – write a letter to his family which is To Be Opened in the Event of His Death. I spent a great deal of time composing that letter. It contained a joke or two, some reminiscences, and an inordinate amount of sound, boring advice. I wrote it in longhand, of course, and when it was sealed in its fancy vellum envelope I placed it in my filing cabinet with the insurance policies. Since then, I have been acutely aware of its existence every time I go to the cabinet for my tax returns, or whatever. It has been a baleful presence in the room, like the lingering smell of something turned rancid. In the same drawer, as it happens,

I keep my shotgun cartridges. The gun, a 12-bore, made me nervous, and I got rid of it some months ago. There's no knowing what a fellow may do if he gets drunk and depressed and there's a gun in the house. Well, one does accept after a while that actually *being* middle-aged isn't anything like as awesome as *becoming* it. And similarly, I guess, death itself won't be as terrifying as the dying of it. Today I decided to destroy the letter. I read it through again before I burned it. The style was not mine; the thoughts expressed were excruciatingly banal. I could have had nothing but contempt for any child of mine who acted upon such limp advice as I offered. It may well be that one day I will write a note to them beginning, 'I have done what I have done because . . .' But if I do I'll not require an envelope, vellum or no. One reaches a point beyond which it is impossible to write ridiculous letters.

COSHER AND THE SEA

It looked as if Cosher wouldn't come. Anyway, I'd wait a bit longer at the side of the empty road. I could see both ends of the village from where I sat. He might come from Purvis Corner, if he'd called on his brother on his way home from work, but if he'd gone straight home, he'd come from the lane by the College Café. Sometimes when I didn't wait, he came just as I reached my house, and then my mother called me in. When that happened, I used to sit by my window and watch him cross the road, giving cigarettes to girls. Half an hour more, then, I'd give him. I climbed to the top of the tank traps and hung upside down from the top pipe. In the classroom, we had a picture of bats hanging like that – three of them in an old dead tree that looked like a dusty top hat. I imagined fur round my eyes as I looked toward the beach. There was a high bank of shingle between the tank traps and the sea; I couldn't remember what the water looked like, because the beach on the south coast of England had been mined and closed seven years before, when the war started. I was only three at the time. At high tide on a windy day, our house was drenched with the thrown spray. Sometimes we could just glimpse the top of a very big wave. Sometimes the sea was so rough that it blew up a mine or two, and then I wouldn't go home, because my father would be crying again, thinking of the day his brother went to get firewood from the bungalow with the smashed windows. Charlie Page had come to our house and told us how the mine had exploded just as they were leaving with their bundles of wood. Charlie was not ten yards away, and he hadn't been touched. Hanging there, I pretended that the sky was the sea and the moving clouds were waves.

All day in school I'd been looking forward to seeing Cosher. He wasn't much taller than I was, but he was nearly fifteen and had left school the previous summer. He shaved and smoked and swore and knew what soldiers did to girls in the empty house when it was dark. One night, he said, he'd take me to see. In my top pocket I still had the airplane cards he'd given me the day before. Cosher had the whole set, even the rare Russian planes. Most evenings, we'd go to the American airmen's billets behind Simpson's barn and beg for empty packets of Sweet Caporals and tear the airplane pictures off the back. I wouldn't go on my own, because some of the airmen used to drink meths and lie about the floor as if they were dead. My father had some in a tin to wash paintbrushes. Cosher asked me to steal it to swap for sweets and cigarettes, but I wouldn't, because I knew about the paint. If he came that evening, it would be too late to walk as far as the billets. I was very disappointed. The sea was the sky again, and I climbed down and rubbed away the orange rust from my hands and legs.

I looked up the road, but still he wasn't coming. It was the summer, and the clocks had been put on two hours. It wouldn't be dark for two hours yet, but before long I'd have to go in and wash and go to bed and watch the street lamp slowly grow stronger than the sunset. The lamps had been turned on again a few weeks before. The night they were switched on, my father and the neighbours made bonfires with the blackout curtains. Somebody had saved some fireworks since before the war, and we had to stand back while they were let off. Cosher brought some Very lights he had found in the shipyard. They went higher than the Roman candles and made twice as much noise. If he came, we could go to his shed for half an hour and look at his collection. Only a few of us knew what was in that padlocked shed.

The first time I went there, about a year before, it was with the Hood twins, Reg and Jim. They were bigger than Cosher, but a year younger and still at school. I had to kneel down and cross my heart never to tell anybody about the shed. They all pressed down with both hands on my head while I promised. They took me inside. Cosher placed every item of his collection, one by one, on the bench. The cartridges first. There were two matchboxes full of tiny copper .22 bullets. Forty-two – he counted them. And then two biscuit tins of mixed .303s and .301s, most of them dull but some bright gold that he'd polished with Bluebell. I knew all about these bullets, and the larger Bren and Sten cartridges, because there were fifty rounds of each sort kept in the corner cupboard at home, together with the Home Guard rifles and other guns my father had. It was the large shells that I liked best, with the thick brass rims at the bottom; Cosher placed these at the back and arranged the smaller ones in descending order in neat platoons. Then he showed us how to take the bullet out of a live shell, holding it in the vice and easing the nipped bullet out with pincers. He did this with several different kinds of shell. He tipped the cordite out of each on to a piece of tissue paper; sometimes the cordite was in little sticks like waxed matches, and

sometimes it was in little circles like confetti. We went outside and watched Cosher lay a trail with the stick cordite
along his garden path. He struck a match and put it to the
end one, and the little bright flame raced almost as far as
the shed door. And then we went in again, because his old
mother was looking through the curtains, and he bolted the
door behind us and showed us the rest. There was a dummy
hand grenade and a yellow-finned smoke bomb and some
black clips. And there was an ostrich egg that his brother
had sent him, painted red. It had a hole in the top to pour
the confetti cordite in. The stick cordite he kept in a jam
jar.

If he came, we could sit in the shed and look at the shells
and talk about the fires we used to make and the camouflaged
camps we erected near the anti-aircraft guns. We still went
sometimes to the camps, but the guns had been taken away
and we were allowed to go to the deserted concrete emplace-
ments; it wasn't much fun creeping through the long grass
now. All we ever found in the ditches where the petrol cans
used to be were damp, ripped magazines with photographs
of nude women. Cosher used to fold up the pictures and
put them in his wallet. Nothing was the same. We'd scoured
the sites of all the crashed planes near the airfield and on
the hills, but there were no more curled bits of aluminium
or slivers of Perspex to polish and carve into brooches or
crucifixes for our mothers. We'd collected every last strip of
tinfoil that had been dropped for radar interference, every
burned-out incendiary bomb, every propaganda leaflet, every
discarded forage cap. The shed was full. The petrol cans
had to be kept outside. We just sat in the shed, knowing the
collection was complete. There was nothing left to do except
go to the billets so that I could get the full set of airplane

pictures to lay out side by side with Cosher's. I only wanted three more, and if he came that evening he might have them.

I looked again along the wide, empty road. Old Mr Daughtery, our next-door neighbour, was striding toward me with his broom on his shoulder, one foot on each side of the white line in the middle. There was never any traffic now. All the tanks and Bren-gun carriers and armoured cars had gone. And the private cars were still in their garages on soft, perished tyres. Mr Daughtery was quiet these days when he came home. There was never much for him to sweep up on the roads, nothing for him to complain about. The tanks used to crush the kerb-stones, and the convoys left him with the job of tidying up, which nobody else would bother to do. Once, a German bomber crashed near the bridge, and it had taken him a week to clean the mud off the road. When he had gone past me, I could see nobody else.

And then Cosher came into sight – unmistakably Cosher, on his roller skates, passing the cottages with long, powerful strides. But tonight there was an urgency in his skating; it was jerky and stabbing, with none of his usual careless elegance, none of his tricks and flourishes. When he was near me, he crouched down to glide up to where I was sitting and stopped by pointing his toes in and hanging round my neck.

'They've opened the beach at Chandler's Corner,' he said. 'I'm going to get Reg and Jim. Wait for us.' And off he went.

But they all had skates and I didn't. If I waited, I knew they wouldn't wait for me. As soon as Cosher had got into his stride again, making for the Hood twins' house, I disobeyed him for the first time and ran as fast as I could away from him toward Chandler's Corner. I didn't look round as I went past my house; I knew my mother would be watching for me. I heard her call, but I ran on. All the way along the road, people were coming out of their houses and walking in the direction of Chandler's. I ran through them and wouldn't stop until I saw the breach that had been made in the tank traps, but then I walked, seeing the crowds queuing up on the shingle and filing past the policemen and the soldiers who were piling up the dismantled pipes and nuts and bolts. I saw, too, boys in my class at school, boys of my age. We formed a pack and pushed through.

At the top of the shingle bank, just through the opening, we stopped for a second or two, not knowing which way to go. We looked at each other and then we laughed – there was only one way *to* go. We ran straight toward the sea.

The tide was right out. Our shoes filled with little stones as we half ran and half slid down the shingle. When we reached the sand, we kicked off our shoes and socks and ran across the wormcasts and bits of seaweed, and flung shells at the wind and ground starfish under our heels. We piled weed on our heads and pretended to be Neptune, kicked up the standing water, skimmed stones, waded up to our waists in the sea. We found dead fish and tossed them where the girls were hanging back by the breakwaters. We threw ourselves down and rolled over and over until we felt the wet through our clothes. We filled our mouths with salt water from our cupped hands and spat it out. We dug with rusks of driftwood and chased the whitebait over the sand and into the sea. When I was too tired to do anything else and it was getting dark, I sat on the stones and watched the birds whose names I didn't know. There was a big, dark-green one that sat on a stump in the sea and kept diving in for fish. And

many little ones that flew together low over the water. I
remember them so vividly – the cormorants and the sand
martins – and over the bay the cliffs at Beachy Head. I
suppose I must have sat there a good half hour, growing up
into a boy, grinding a stone on a stone, pulling a yellow poppy
to shreds, watching the big boys, Reg, Jim, and Cosher, as
they walked on their own along the sands. They were carrying their silly skates. They called me, but I wouldn't follow
them.

IN DUE SEASON

It was not long before midnight. They had come to bed just after eleven, had read for a little while, made love for a little while, and now they were reading again. Celia had to finish her thriller before the mobile library arrived at lunchtime next day in the village square. Henry was studying a pre-war manual on vegetables. It was the first day of spring, a Sunday. Henry, that afternoon, had planted early potatoes and Jerusalem artichokes and sown seeds of parsnips, carrots and broad beans.

During their love-making, his mind had been on the garden and the greenhouse; should he, this year, try to raise a few exotic items – exotic, that is, in England – like capsicums, kohl rabi, couve tronchuda? He liked the sound of the last of these. *When the outer leaves have been used*, he read, *there remains the heart, for cooking cabbage fashion; it is tastier for having been touched by frost.* In his imagination, it was already high summer. Shirtless, he was pushing a hoe between his immaculate rows of couve tronchuda. What did the vegetable look like? The manual provided no illustration. The brief description (between *Compost Heap* and *Corn Salad, or Lamb's Lettuce*) was tantalising. *A substitute is not necessarily an inferior. This certainly holds good in the case of couve tronchuda, otherwise known as Portugal cabbage; the big white, fleshy ribs of the outer leaves are delicious when used as seakale.* Well, whatever its appearance, it was worth growing for its name alone. He would enjoy being asked what it was – though Celia, no doubt, would enjoy supplying the English name: a monoglot, after twenty years of marriage she delighted in deflating his delight in parading his knowledge of languages. What had *her* mind been on, he wondered, during their routine and almost cursory embraces? Their simultaneous climax had been, as usual, satisfactory; but satisfactory was not, in matters of the heart, ever satisfactory. The word, in the context of the bedroom, meant the exact opposite of its dictionary definition. At forty, did one have to accept that adequate was enough? Henry shuddered, remembering the feel of her brushed nylon nightdress against his roughened hands. He'd had to fight against stinging nettles, ground elder and the intractable roots that spread from an apple tree, to get the plot ready for planting. He wished she'd taken the nightdress off, wished she'd commented, afterwards, on the fact that he'd caressed her with the smooth back of his hand. When the outer leaves have been used, there remains the heart.

'Henry, are you sure that bonfire's safe?' she said to him. He guessed, and ascertained, that she'd reached the end of a chapter. Thirty or forty pages to go; about half an hour to relish. If he'd not intruded on her, she'd have finished the book by now and they'd both have been asleep.

'Of course it's safe. All the dry stuff had burned up by the time I put the car away. That heap of weeds I piled on top was too wet to do more than smoulder. Probably out by now.'

'Have a look. Please, Henry. There's a wind getting up.

One stray spark and you can kiss the garage goodbye. I can't imagine why you didn't build the fire at the other end of the garden.'

'It'll be all right,' he said. There was goodness in bonfire ashes. A barrow load for the tomatoes in the greenhouse; another load raked in above the potatoes. Natural potash to leach down.

'Or you could have left it to dry out for a bit. There's no hurry.'

She was treasuring the book against her breast, like a kitten.

'Please.'

'Okay, okay.'

He crossed the room to the window, came back, hunted for his pyjama trousers at the bottom of the bed, put them on, went to the window again and parted the curtains. She'd been right about the wind. It had nosed under the fire, rekindling the chars and embers which now glowed like a brazier in the dark. Little flarings dropped from the edges of the soggy heap and a sudden gust sent a shower of sparks high in the air. Henry watched them drift like a dusting of snow across the lawn as they whirled into ashes. Damn her for being right, he thought; for being always in the right.

'Why bother putting on your pyjama bottoms?' she said. 'Nobody overlooks that window.' Come to think of it, he hadn't bothered taking off his pyjama top. But then, neither had she.

'Cold,' he said, not turning round. 'Be a ground frost before morning.'

'Is it out?'

'It soon will be. Just a few bits of dead rosewood among the nettles. Get on with your book. I'll keep an eye on it.'

'I told you about that wind.'

'It's blowing away from the house. Away from the garage.'

'I'll not be able to sleep so long as there's a single spark,' she said. She flicked a page over. He heard her cracking the spine of the book.

'Just relax. If necessary, I'll go down and turn the hose on it. Promise. Right now, I just want to watch it from here. I like watching a bonfire. Always did.' He sat down on the end of the bed, put on his socks and slippers, and then, picking up his dressing-gown, went back to the window. A band of flame, a foot across, was racing up the windward side of the weed pile; it tapered abruptly and extinguished, reminding Henry of those animated maps they use in films to show the movements of armies. Another sortie of yellow consumed a dangling strand of nettle. Sniping flares picked off skeletal leaves that fell and rose and fell again in brilliant curlicues. The fire was making enough light now for Henry to be able to make out the smallest details of its activity. It was making inroads, with each breath of the wind, into the slushing armful of ivy he'd dumped on the blazing pyramid of apple prunings. Under the bonfire – Henry had built it on top of an old bed-spring set on bricks – was a thick layer of ashes pulsating white, red, white: the gleeds (his grandmother's word) and the underheat. All night long it would burn, sometimes jogging, sometimes sprinting. If the wind turned round, the paint on the garage doors would blister and bubble up into flammable weals. There was no rain about; the stars were fierce and blue beyond the smoke and the orchard. He would have to attend to it before long.

'The soft stuff would have made good compost,' she said. 'It's a waste, burning it. What that garden needs is good humus.'

'Potash is good.'

'Compost is better. All that goodness going up in smoke. It would have rotted down by the back end of summer.' She lit a cigarette, her gas lighter hissing. Right again.

'I like a good fire to mark the end of winter. There'll be daffodils out by the end of the week. We've never had such a show of quince blossom. I should have sown some lettuce.'

'You're in too much of a rush. The ground's still clammy and cold. Needs a week or two of sun.'

'Go back to your murder.'

'Not till you've doused that fire. I shall, if you don't.'

'I will. I will.'

But he would douse it in his own good time. The garden by now was full of flickering light that cast no shadow; it glanced, danced, along the high brick wall whenever the smallest flame licked out of the fire, the way that the merest sound carried along the smooth surface of the Whispering Gallery at St Paul's Cathedral. Summer nights, he enjoyed watching electrical storms from this window. Distant lightning, as it surgeoned out the throbbing tumours of August weather, flickered among the roses and over the grass with a similar mystery; the thunder would be too far away to hear, and no rain would fall. Henry, an incompetent gardener, was full of ambitions for their third of an acre. What arbours of wisteria, what pergolas, urns, hanging baskets and formal patterns of herbs he would design if only Celia would enthuse with him! There, beyond the square plot of artichokes (Jerusalem: a corruption of *girasole*, a sunflower) he would have a rustic seat entwined with honeysuckle, sweet woodbine, if Celia hadn't earmarked the site for one of her compost heaps. She it was who knew best how, and when, things could, and should, be done. Anything grew for her. By the last week in October she would have filled the deep-freeze cram-full of beans, peas, blackberries and apple purée; she would have harvested the onions, hanging them on long strands of raffia from the conservatory ceiling; and it was Celia, frankly, who would lift the potatoes and the artichokes and put them in sacks and find cool places to store them. She kept up with the work that had to be done: weeding, mulching, feeding, watering, thinning out, propagating – all in due season. She kept to no calendar but that of the shifts of England's climate, crumbling a handful of soil, squinting up at the clouds and the breaks in the clouds, fondling a plant as one might fondle a child.

Henry accepted this. But at the end of winter, the end of the third week of every March, he spent a weekend slogging at the earth whether or not it was ready. He stared down at the trim rectangles of newly-turned ground where he'd dug, raked, planted and sowed. Yes, the carrot seeds might rot and yes, the potatoes might have been left another fortnight to sprout in the shed: but it was worth gambling a few pennies to fight against nature and to establish a foothold in spring. What did it matter that the dribbled seeds were in the clutch of the frost he could see by his firelight? If some should survive – enough to provide, in early summer, one serving for dinner – then all his hours of furious labour would be vindicated. Henry looked at his hands. They were scratched, splintered, throbbing with nettle stings; there was blood in his nails. He was tired, fulfilled, more than moderately happy.

'It'll be a wonderful summer,' he said, his back to her.

'What makes you say that?'

'I don't know. I just think it's our turn for a good summer. We ought to have a fig tree.'

'There's nowhere we could have one. They're risky, figs.'
'I don't care. I'd like one. I'd like to see one grow, that's all.'
'A plum tree would be better. A nice Victoria plum.'
'You said we haven't the room.'
'If we had.'

The fire was sullen again, as it had been when he'd left it in the dusk. It was still alive in its embers, though, and inexorably drying off the matted foliage that could not choke it. Good bonfires have their periods of retrenchment: *reculer pour mieux sauter*, Henry thought. If he left it, by three in the morning it would be on the march again, a threat.

He glanced at her as he opened the bedroom door. Half a dozen pages to go. She would enjoy them all the more, knowing that he was going to put the fire out. He passed the children's bedrooms on the landing (she would have been anxious on their account) and caught a glimpse of himself in the mirror at the foot of the stairs. What kind of idiotic gardener he was, to have to attend to urgent chores at midnight in dressing-gown and carpet slippers!

He walked to the fire along the path of light shining down from the bedroom window. The grass was brittle with frost. Above the garden wall he saw the momentary beam of a car's headlights, milky with smoke. If the summer was good he would spend a couple of nights bream fishing at the harbour; he liked best those July nights when the skin of the sea is taut, unpuckered, when the smoke of his cigarette rises straight and the intermittent flash from the lightship spreads like a balm along the water. He would come home at first light and walk about in the garden, the roses at their best, the late clematis beginning to open, the peaches warm as flesh. Maybe he'd take Celia to visit some of the great gardens of England. Sissinghurst was his particular favourite, answering his need for what was eccentric, wayward, distinctive, capricious. He thought of the avenue of Lombardy poplars there, which (so he had been told) Harold Nicolson had brought home from Italy as saplings, in his sponge bag. Something of Sissinghurst could be transplanted, surely, into this prosaic and workaday patch of ground? Some daft, romantic touch. He'd grow that couve tronchuda, by God, whether or not it took up space Celia would want for Brussels sprouts. And he'd have his way over the fig tree – though where it could be put he really did not know. Yet.

He kicked the bonfire over. The green stuff was hot and full of steam and gouts of smoke. He turned on the hose and his hands were suddenly numbed with icy water. The ashes hissed, and as the heavy spurts and jets thudded among the feathery patterns, Henry shivered and stamped his feet against the onrush of cold and the utter cheerlessness of the sodden chars turning over and over under pressure of the water.

He was surprised, as he turned off the tap and glanced up at the window, to see her standing there. Was she checking to see that he'd done the job properly? He coiled the hose on to its drum; took a fork and spread the rubbish over a wide area. He wanted her to see, beyond all doubt, that it was harmless; wanted her to be at ease. When he looked up again, she was not there.

And, by the time he'd put the hose and the fork away, she'd left the garden in darkness. He imagined her behind the blank window, plumping her pillow, turning her back on the empty half of the bed. She needed her sleep. Mondays were always frantic for Celia. He shuffled back to the house and, after he'd bolted the door, he stood for several minutes

in the warmth of the kitchen. The smell of cold smoke was
in his hair, his clothes. He sniffed at his sleeve, felt the damp
cuff at his cheek. He poured himself a large scotch, sat down
by the stove and read the leading article in the *Observer:* at
breakfast, he'd scarcely opened the paper before starting
work with the spade. Then, guessing that by now Celia
would be fast asleep, he climbed the stairs, took off his
dressing-gown and hung it up behind the bedroom door.

'You must be frozen through,' she said, as he got into
bed.

'Sorry,' he said. 'Did I wake you?'

'I was watching you. I could see how hard the frost is.
The wind's dying down. The water must have been like ice.
Your poor hands.'

'I'm all right.'

'You work so hard.'

'Not to much effect. You were right about those seeds.
Should have waited.'

'I didn't mean that. I mean work *generally*. I don't know
what I mean.'

She put her arm over him, and Henry took hold of her
hand. It felt colder than his own.

Her arm was warm, though, and as he traced it, cradled
her elbow, turned towards her and held her shoulder, it
dawned on him that she had taken off her nightdress and
had lain there waiting for him.

ELGAR COUNTRY

The afternoon, though bitterly cold, was made cheerful by the first sunshine since Christmas. Its brilliance flooded the beechwood, discovering frailest nuances of colour among remnants of snow; silver of the trees' smooth trunks was overlaid with a thin wash of golden-green. There was no wind. Sounds carried from long distances, undistorted, up the hill. Somewhere a muntjac barked, pheasants crowed drily, and far off in the valley an expensive car was growling through its gears.

Chris and Barbara Groves had left their Renault beside the road at the top of the wood. Now they were a hundred feet below it, following a bridle path they knew would lead to a village still out of sight. Their plan was to have a cup of tea there and then to climb back by a different way.

They hadn't spoken since Chris had turned off the engine. 'This is Elgar country,' he'd said, looking away from her and over the beeches towards the Weald. 'I know,' Barbara had said. They'd sat there a few moments more while he wound his scarf round and round his neck. 'It's where he wrote the Cello Concerto,' he'd said. 'I know that, too,' she'd replied. 'You told us all before.' Then they'd slammed the doors and begun the descent. The party of rooks that had lifted, cawed, and fluttered like black banners, had settled again, and the hillside was quiet as wool.

Chris walked a couple of paces behind his wife. It felt strange, being quite alone with her in a lonely place. There was no one else to share the wood with them. It was a weekday; his office in the City was closed for its bi-annual painting, and Barbara had suggested this drive down to Sussex. He was beginning to wish that they'd gone somewhere jolly and crowded. They could have stopped at Kingston, say, or Richmond, and enjoyed the winter sunshine strolling beside the Thames or browsing along busy shopping streets.

For almost twenty years they'd had their two children with them whenever they had a day out in the country. When Patrick and Maureen were still very small (there was less than a twelvemonth between them) Chris had carried them on his shoulders or towed them in their pushchair up and down dirt tracks, along beaches, beside streams. As they grew up, they had trailed plaintively, petulantly, behind with their mother as Chris beat a path through wet thickets, round patches of standing water. Town kids, he maintained, needed to stretch their legs now and again in the fresh air; and nearly always it was Sussex he took them to – the county where he had lived as a child. He pitied Patrick and Maureen for being born and bred Londoners simply because their father was obliged to work there. So, even through their adolescence, Chris had insisted on their *tagging along* of a Sunday afternoon whenever it wasn't actually raining; it did them no good at all, he said, to be stuck indoors all the time with those vile pop records. And, with bad grace, they had continued to tag along – in unsuitable shoes and chattering endlessly about *the Charts* while he tried to interest them in things he knew about.

Now they had both left home, not without acrimony, and he and Barbara were left with each other. Anything he might say in this remote corner of southern England would be said to her alone.

And there was nothing he could say, except what was important: too important to be uttered on this abrupt hill path, surrounded by leafless beech trees in which scarcely a bird sang more than a brief snatch of its bleak winter song. But where would anything be said that mattered? In bed? In the car? Where, for that matter, were trivial things said? And *when* were they said, lately, since the two kids had gone? Chris picked up a piece of rotted branch to fling at the silence; it broke as he threw it, and the two halves fell, thud, thud, in the quiltings of God knew how many seasons' leafmould. Small talk ought to be easy between a man and his wife, he thought. He didn't have to feel awkward and embarrassed with her, like a boy on his first date. (The first time he had taken her out, he remembered, he had kissed her under trees like these.)

It was different in the house. In the house the television was always on, or they had their books and magazines to withdraw into between fragments of ritualised and necessary communication; did he want a cup of coffee, could she tell him what had become of the nail scissors? Different in town, too, where check-out assistants, traffic wardens and passers-by acted as the unwitting intermediaries to their conversation, closing the circuit that, somehow, had been fragmenting over the years. And, true, they got on well enough together when guests at friends' dinner tables or at cocktail parties. Out here, though, surrounded by wildness, it was as though they needed some stranger – a spinster lady with her terrier, a game warden looking to his pheasants – before either of them could be articulate.

27

He was still walking behind her, a few inches higher than she. Looking down at the crown of her head he noticed how grey her blond hair was becoming; and the lambswool lining of her coat collar was a dingier white, even, than that of old snow. He couldn't, in all conscience, pass comment on facts like that.

In the days when the children were still with them, he would have gathered the three of them together and addressed them collectively. Here, at this bend in the track, he would have made them stop. He would have told them about the plant called butcher's broom, about where wrens make their nests, about Elgar writing his last great work hereabouts after the end of the Great War. How ridiculous it would be, dishing out such a miscellany to her on her own!

She looked, as ever, strong and well, the bloom of good health on her cheek as she turned to face him.

He loved her. But she already knew that.

'Surely you remember, don't you?' she said.

'Remember what?'

'That day here. Telling us about that composer.'

Chris nodded, sighed. 'Palmy days,' he said. They walked on.

That must have been seven, eight, years since. He recalled Patrick's still unbroken voice calling from a rhododendron clump as he chased after that disobedient mongrel they briefly owned; Maureen's screaming tantrum when she tore her dress on a bramble. There had been the not unpleasant smell of horse dung on their shoes when they reached home and he quizzed them on the day's new facts. God! what a bore he'd been. Was it to be wondered at that his son and daughter had got the hell out at the earliest opportunity?

'Was it unbearably irritating, Bar?' he found himself saying.

'Was what irritating, love?'

'The way I was always lecturing you all like some clapped-out schoolmaster.'

'Not to me. I liked it when you told us things.'

'The kids, then.'

'Shouldn't think so. But you can't ever tell with kids.'

On the lower, gentler slopes now, they entered a young plantation of chestnut. Tractors had been working there; tyre-ruts, filled with water, had iced over. It had felt warmer among the mature trees. Barbara, beside her husband, saw him shudder, pinched with the sudden cold. He'd put himself on a severe diet recently and lost about twenty pounds too quickly. How gaunt he looked, how much older, and how shabbily his clothes hung on him. She'd preferred him as he had been ever since she'd known him – when they were still in their teens: chubby, exuberant, at ease in his battered tweeds and duffel coat.

'Let's step it out,' she said to him. 'Come on, we both need a hot drink inside us.' She was going to try and persuade him to eat something, too; but she guessed that he would remain adamant. There was likely to be nothing on the menu that was not against his self-inflicted régime. He would watch her consume a toasted tea-cake, or a buttered bun, or a pastry oozing double cream. Barbara's beauty had coarsened since she'd entered her forties, but her figure had thickened out only slightly. It bothered her that Chris, her ample and voracious man, was turning into such a withered and joyless ascetic. He grudged himself calories, laughter, words even. She strode on, the way *he* used to stride ahead, jinking between patches of frozen mud and ducking athletically under overhanging branches.

The village spread before them: black-and-white half-timbered cottages, a couple of pubs, half a dozen little shops all clustered around a church with a shingled steeple. Somewhere there was bound to be a tea-shop. Chris imagined it – a quaint interior, darkish, cramped, with gateleg tables and Windsor chairs; the kind of establishment they'd seldom had the courage to patronise when the children were small and boisterous or when they were older and gauche. In short, it would be the sort of place where couples, freed of their families, took their decorous afternoon tea. High-Tory Sussex abounded with such tea-shops; prissily genteel, they catered for retired gentlefolk in the main – military buffers in deerstalker hats and their skinny wives in thick beige stockings and brogues. Over the Willow-pattern crockery, among the horse-brasses, with the mingled scents of hot crumpets and furniture polish, he and Barbara would whisper inconsequentially until, after their second cup, he left a frantic tip for some hard-faced and snooty waitress. In that atmosphere of disapprobation verging upon candid hostility, they would have no chance to say what needed saying.

'Bar,' he said, as they reached the paved road. 'I wonder how they're getting on?'

'They'll survive.'

'I wish they hadn't gone. Not the way they did.'

'It's done now.'

'All that bitterness. I needn't have acted as I did. I didn't want us to fall out.' He lit a cigarette, taking his time. He couldn't weep – not here, in the street.

'They'll soon learn, love. They had to be told a few hard facts of life.'

'That's all I ever seemed to do – give them facts.'

'Hard facts, I said.'

'Not written. Not phoned.'

'Don't talk about it now, Chris. Later.'

'We can't keep putting it off and off. It all needs talking through. Our kids have gone, Bar. Gone, and no word. I'd want to say I was sorry. I didn't mean to be hurtful.'

There were old men in gardens now, housewives carrying shopping baskets home, small children just released from the village school. 'Later, Chris,' she said to him. 'Please don't go on about it now.'

They stopped to gaze into the window of the first shop they reached – an Arts-and-Crafts store full of the wares made by local people. Chris looked balefully at rows of misshapen, gaudy or mud-coloured pottery, racks of chunkily knitted garments, wood-carvings vaguely resembling herons, seals, elephants.

'If you don't watch out,' he said, 'I'll buy you that parody milk-jug.'

He'd made her grin; he grinned himself.

The tea-shop, next door, was called 'The Robin-à-Tiptoe'. It had a bow window, from which a dozen or so china dogs stared at them.

'The hell with it,' Chris said. 'I'm not going to be condescended to by some hoity-toity dowager. I've got a much better idea.'

He took her into the grocer's shop opposite. She watched him select a pork pie, some fancy cakes and a half-bottle of single-malt whisky.

'I'll have a bite from the pie,' he said, once they were outside.

'I'm ravenous,' she said. 'Can't wait to get back to the car.'

'Nor can I. We'll find somewhere to sit down, out of the cold.'

They sat in the back pew of the parish church. Barbara spread the food between them on her silk scarf. Chris unstoppered the bottle and took a long, grateful slug.

'Not exactly reverential,' she said, as he passed the whisky to her.

'Still an *agape* for all that.'

'*Agape?*'

'Love-feast. Greek.'

'Oh.'

'I'm at it again. Telling you facts. Drink up.'

She did so; and he, calculating his calorie intake, cut out a quarter of the pie with his pen-knife. Whisky, a hundred; pie, a hundred and twenty-five, say. He noticed how the sun, now low in the sky, streamed through the stained-glass window behind them and on to his wife's hair, cheek, hands, as she sat sideways in the pew. It had been a very long time indeed since they'd last been together in a church.

'Can you bear it if I quote something at you?' he said to her.

'Quote away, provided you don't keep me from my éclair.'

'*Rose-bloom fell on her hands, together prest,*
And on her silver cross soft amethyst,
And on her hair a glory, like a saint.'

'Shelley,' she said, dropping crumbs of chocolate.

'Keats. And you butted in before I got to the most complimentary bit.'

'A compliment would go down well. This cake's delicious.'

'*She seemed a splendid angel, newly drest.*'

'In a tatty old car-coat only fit for the boy scout jumble sale?'

'I reckon you're splendid, Bar. Even if your hands are pressed round an éclair or a bottle of malt.'

'Bet the girl in the poem didn't have grey hair.'

'You'll do.'

His words echoed, then the church fell silent again. They had begun talking in hushed, stage whispers and had finished speaking aloud. Barbara giggled, sensing Chris's self-consciousness.

'You're not so bad yourself. What was she up to, this splendid angel?'

'Waiting for a vision of her lover.' He barely more than mouthed the last syllables, glancing towards the altar as he did so.

'Her what?'

'*Lover.* In fact, he came in person after she'd said her prayers and gone to bed.'

'And?'

'And they set to and ate prodigious quantities of exotic candies and fruits.'

'Is *that* all?' She pulled a wry face, selected a custard tart.

'No, of course not. But that's all Keats could say. Ostensibly, they just tucked into their feast, but there's no doubt what the poet wanted us to read into it. They had it away. The lines sound like – '

'Like what? Come on – don't be coy.'

'Well, like sounds of sex. Physical love. Marvellously accurate. Listen –

With jellies soother than the creamy curd,

And lucent syrops, tinct with cinnamon – How about that?'

'Really, Christopher Groves – whatever next? Swigging hard liquor and chanting soft old porn in the house of God! You'll be struck dead. Pass me that bottle.'

Chris remembered an afternoon (how old were they then: seventeen, eighteen?) when they'd run from the rain into the church where, in fact, they were subsequently married. It was in the summer; the high Norman nave had swallows skimming, aglint as sapphires, between the columns and in and out of the clerestory lancets. A Saturday, it must have been. The chancel steps were decorated with white flowers; there had been a wedding. Chris recalled in fine detail how, for the first time, he cupped Barbara's breasts as they sat in the north aisle. She had been praying, her long golden hair falling strand by strand over the pew she rested on. 'Not in here, Chris,' she'd said, her face flushed. 'How could you?' He'd said, 'But I love you, Bar. It's all right.' And then, for the rest of the day, they'd pursued one of their silent quarrels, traipsing around the town glumly until it was time for them to take their separate buses home. Not talking had been, as long ago as that, a form of communication for them: he guessed what she was thinking, and she, too, speculated. 'I suppose it was all right, Chris,' she'd finally said at her bus stop. 'I'd supposed that you supposed that,' he'd said. Now here they were, a quarter of a century on. He smiled at her.

'Know what I'm thinking?' he said.

'That time in St Mary's when we were sheltering?'

'Right.' It still worked.

Barbara gathered up the crumbs, the uneaten quarters of pie, wrapped them in her scarf and put them in her handbag. Chris pocketed the remains of the whisky; they'd drunk about half of it. 'It's not raining today,' he said, pushing the great oak door open for her. 'Good job too,' she said. 'Goodness knows what you'd have got up to if it had been.'

*   *   *

34

They were half-way back up the hill before either felt the need to talk any more. Chris sensed that Barbara would bring up the topic of their children when it suited her to; obviously, she had something important to say on the subject, and she was still trying to work out the best way of expressing it. 'Later,' she'd said down in the village. The word was a kind of contract.

He wondered where his son and daughter were. They were sensible kids, old enough to fend for themselves. They weren't likely to come to harm. They had several hundred pounds each in the bank. Probably they were staying with friends in some university city, learning how to wash their own clothes, how to cook simple meals on a gas ring. They would be slightly uncomfortable; and that was all to the good. Surely to God they had no doubt that he loved them – for all the hard things he'd had to say about their general fecklessness?

The sun had set, and the woods were darkening. The night was going to be very cold. The melody of the slow movement of Elgar's concerto entered Chris's mind as they turned the last bend of the path before the final hundred yards or so. He knew every one of its sixty bars of almost unbearable sadness, could visualise the agonised face of Tortelier as he played them. Each note had been kindled among these beeches, somewhere, when Elgar poured out all his melancholy and despair for broken Europe.

'It's not so bad, is it?' Barbara said.

'What isn't?' She'd interrupted the movement in the last bar but one.

'Being on our own again. The house quiet. I've loved today.'

'Me, too. I could just finish off that pork pie. We're fine. We'll survive.'

In the car they sat until the day was quite gone, eating, smoking, sipping a little more of the whisky. Barbara wound down her window, and in the stillness they could hear the rustle of deer passing quite close. Then, abruptly, Chris started the engine, reversed on to the road, moved gently towards the bend.

'I can guess,' he said, 'why you suggested we should come out for the day. Plain as daylight.'

'All right, mind-reader. Tell me.'

'They've been in touch, haven't they? Probably phoned a day or two back when I was at work. Said they wanted to come home and collect some of their stuff today, thinking I'd not be there. But they hadn't known about the office being re-decorated. So you had to get me out in case we all had another row. Correct?'

'Partly, love. How did you guess?'

'Did the same myself, didn't I, when I was their age? For heaven's sake – I told the kids the story many a time. About how I got my mother to take my father out shopping while I slunk in and collected some clean shirts. You've been doing their laundry for them, haven't you, Bar? I'll lay money on it. The two of them are living somewhere in London, right? Three or four stops away by Tube. Are they okay, Bar? Did they sound happy?'

'They're fine. Of course they are. But they feel terrible about all that fracas we had. They want, more than anything else, to make it up. I don't think they'll be coming back home to live. But Chris – they do, desperately, want to see you. *Us*. Promise not to be angry if I tell you something else?'

'What could make me angry?'

'They're afraid of you. They don't know how to talk to you.'

*   *   *

36

He changed into top, now that he was on the flat. London was an hour and a half away. Afraid? Of him? But he was afraid of *them*. Didn't know how to talk to *them*, for Christ's sake. Maybe he should write to them. At once, he began composing his letter. How do you write such a letter, he wondered.

'Are you still with me, Chris?'

'What?'

'I left a note on the kitchen table for them. Said I'd phone about six o'clock to let them know if all's well, so to speak. Do you want them to be there waiting for us, or not? If you'd sooner give it a few days more – '

Chris looked at his watch: five forty-five. He turned on the radio, to be sure of an accurate time–check. This side of Guildford they would find a telephone kiosk, and after the call was made (Barbara must make it: he wouldn't know quite what to say) they'd have a leisurely drink in some pub before completing the journey. The kids wouldn't have to mind waiting another twenty minutes while their parents prepared themselves for this unusual encounter, would they? Not that he could rehearse it in his mind beyond the moment when he put his key in the lock. He'd be on his guard not to press them into staying the night. The Tube trains ran very late; if they stayed too late for the last one, well, they could remain if they felt like it. Offhand, he'd be. Cool. He'd enjoy watching them eat a square meal. He thought of his own old man once, spooning pickled onions on to his plate for him. The hell with the diet. He'd eat hearty, too. He felt in his pocket for coins for the phone, handed them to Barbara, and from the car he watched as she dialled their number, pushed in the coins, babbled into the receiver.

37

'They're going to wait,' she said. 'Now, let's change the subject.'

'Agreed. What shall it be?'

'Anything. Lucent syrops. Kissing etcetera in church. Elgar, if you really must.'

'Sod Elgar.'

THE BEDROOM

It was watching a house martin that kept me alone for a while in this room. We'd just had dinner. I ran upstairs to fetch a handkerchief, and there was the bird hovering outside the window. The tips of its wings were almost brushing against the dusty glass for an instant before it disappeared up into its nest under the eaves. Within seconds, I saw the bird again. It fell back into view and, as if following the curve of some invisible slide, skimmed down toward the end of the garden. Almost at once, it was back at the window, to hover and then disappear once more. Its breast had the sheen of white satin. In the May sunshine, the martin was repairing its nest, bringing soft mud from beside the pond. Most years, we have martins and swallows under the eaves; some make entirely new nests, but others make good the ones left from the summer before. I sat down in the armchair I leave my clothes on at night, and watched the bird make a few more journeys.

I'd not sat in that chair since we moved into this house, seven years ago. When we came here from a much smaller house, we bought new furniture for the living room, and this chair was relegated upstairs. It has bare wood arms, a seat of foam rubber, small wings – what is described in salesrooms as a TV chair. I felt comfortable in it; maybe I'd take it down to my study, where its grey fabric would go well with a many-coloured wall of books. But then if I did that I should have to bring up one of the old kitchen chairs to hang my clothes on. This one was perfect for the job – trousers, held by friction, did not slip from its back to the floor; jackets (for I am unusually broad in the chest) were made to measure for its stump wings; the arms were of a convenient height for me when I was lacing shoes. I made a rapid calculation. More than two and a half thousand times I'd draped trousers and jackets on it, flung shirt, tie, and underwear on it. I didn't really need another chair in my study. I'd keep things, after all, as they were.

By now, I'd lost interest in the fluttering bird. I glanced around at the rest of the furniture in this unaccustomed room. There, in one alcove, was my wife's wardrobe. It's a stately, Edwardian item in dark mahogany – tall, panelled, with carved rosettes and brass fittings – which I bought for a few pounds at an auction sale and carried home in sections on top of the car the week we moved in. I'd not appraised its handsomeness since we assembled it, dusted it out, fitted the linen drawer, which smelled of lavender grown in some-one's garden before the Battle of the Somme. I opened the doors, parted my wife's dresses, saw behind them the faded floral pattern of the lining paper – elegant, worth looking at. And in the other alcove was my wardrobe, more workaday, more squat, thirtyish, light oak. I'd been given it by a man dead these five years. It has shelves and drawers on the left-hand side marked 'Shirts,' 'Ties,' 'Hats,' and so on. I keep everything in the wrong compartments. Hatless, I use the top shelf for miscellaneous objects that I don't need but that are too good to throw away – a battery-operated razor, a sunray lamp, a papier-mâché snuffbox containing shirt studs. On the floor of the wardrobe I noticed a pair of walking shoes I'd forgotten I had. It was high time I sorted through my clothes, throwing out the stuff I no longer wore.

It felt extraordinary, poking about in this room in the early evening, being aware of it and its contents in a way I never had been before. Sunlight entered it as it does not in the mornings, picking out unusual surfaces. This was almost somebody else's room. It was the one room in the house we'd not bothered to redecorate. We slept here, washed and dressed, prepared to go out of an evening, made love, sometimes mildly quarrelled in the dark. There, on the bed-side tables, were the books we were currently reading: my wife's Simenon, my Collected Yeats. We were other people when we came into this room. In bed (I studied the design of the Welsh tapestry bed-spread), we were concerned with nothing in the room beyond where our limbs would reach. Otherwise, it was simply an area in which to prepare for another day, another social evening. I thought of myself shaving at that sink, looking into that mirror. There were my toothbrush, my bottle of after-shave, waiting until I should use them next. It was stupid, my being here now, for the wrong reasons. I was astonishing the furniture.

Remembering why I'd come, I took a handkerchief from its drawer. Normally, this would have been a reflex action like blinking the eyes; but now that the martin had kept me here – the bird was still coming and going – I had to stop, and think, and remember to open the drawer marked 'Collars.' Then, for a second or two, I stared at the drawer marked 'Handkerchiefs,' persuading myself that it did indeed contain socks – that I didn't have to check. Outside, on the lawn, my children were arguing over who should bat first in a game of cricket. I moved away from the window, lest they see me up here. They'd call me down, and I didn't want to go yet. I lay on the bed, stared at a vase on the chest of drawers. That vase had never contained flowers, as far as I could recall.

Seven-thirty. As a young bachelor straight out of university, I'd lain like this for twenty minutes or so after cooking some rudimentary snack of an evening. Those London bed-sits! There was never a truly comfortable chair – you had to lie on the bed or sprawl against threadbare cushions on the floor. You'd look up at the grubby ceiling, tracing the map of Asia in the marks of damp. You'd count your pathetic possessions; the suitcase on top of the wardrobe would hold all you owned. There was always somewhere else to go when you were sick of it – similar in its dinginess, but somewhere else. The cooking area and the sink were curtained off with stained and shrivelling plastic hangings, but there was no illusion of having more than one box to be in. The bathrooms were always occupied, or, if not, were festooned with the dripping laundry of other lodgers. There was nowhere to go but elsewhere, paying a week's rent in lieu of notice, and humping the suitcase once more along streets of drab stucco villas, or on to a bus, or down leaf-slippery steps to the Tube. One had lived through that cheerfully enough, twenty years ago. Occasionally (how different it all was then) you might smuggle in some girl, who must be smuggled out again in the early hours before there were even milkmen on the streets; and then those rooms for a week or two would seem special places – always to be remembered, in fine detail, for what had happened in them. But before long it would be another girl, another room, a room whose awfulness had to be borne those few weeks longer than one's loneliness could easily bear.

Later, after the three-week honeymoon room in the Bernese Oberland (that balcony where we had Cape-gooseberry jam for breakfast: the wasps), there were so many two-roomed flats in such a short space of time that I no longer remember each from each, or the order in which they came. Then there was, for a five-year spell during which the children were born, a bedroom in the house I bought so tiny that we had to keep our clothes in a cupboard on the landing. All I can bring back to mind is its tininess. Perhaps it had pink walls.

And now there's this room. Had I not made this impromptu survey this evening, I'd have been hard pressed to give an accurate inventory of what its walls enclose – unlikely as this must seem. As I lay on the bed (I slipped off my shoes) I made another calculation. Probably I spend nine hours out of every twenty-four in here: eight hours of sleep, including love-making; half an hour's reading; thirty minutes more dressing, undressing, grooming. Twenty-three thousand hours I've spent here, and I hardly know the place. Look – the bottom left-hand knob is loose on the dressing-table. There's a dark stain on the carpet near the door.

My wife must see all this in entirely different terms, I realised then. She would be on *intimate* terms with the room in which I was merely a stranger or a guest. I thought of her, weekdays, the house abruptly empty, its rooms all bearing the traces of what we'd been doing in them. What would she be thinking (thinking about me) as she made this bed of ours, replaced the towels, Hoovered the floor, dusted those three alabaster elephants I brought home from America last year? She has to do some of her *living* in here. All those bottles, pots, brushes, and things on the dressing-table; she uses them several times a day. She *sits* there, sees herself in the three mirrors, paints her nails. Nights, while I am already in bed reading, she sits there for minutes after she's finished brushing her hair, doing nothing in particular. Staring. Thinking. From time to time, she suggests we ought to repaper the room, give it a lick of paint. For her sake – for those minutes of the day when she's in here alone – I ought to set to and redecorate.

I feel uneasy – she, alone in this room. Waiting for her hair to dry, listening to the radio, turning the radio off.

I'd sooner the room stayed unmemorable.

The room I was born in was my room until I was eighteen years old. When I was very small, my sister was born in it, only to die within the month. I slept during those weeks, and while my mother raged with puerperal fever, in the living room. Until I was in my teens, I gasped there every summer with my asthma. During the war, in that room, my bed was inside one of those iron air-raid shelters. When my two uncles died – one shot in the African desert, one blown up by a mine on the beach – I was sent into that room to do my crying, while my father hid his eyes in his bedroom, where I couldn't go. I could tell you exactly how many yellow roses there were on that wallpaper, reproduce the pattern of the plywood that lined the fitted cupboard. When there were high tides in November and March, gales could whip the spray off the Channel as far as my window. There was a pear tree outside. Never any pears. A blind tree, my father called it.

Downstairs, the telephone rang while I lay on the bed. My wife called me, but I didn't answer. She would have assumed that I'd gone out for a walk – for what would I be doing up here? I was private, as I could be nowhere else in the house. In my study, in the bathroom, they'd know where to find me, but not here.

This could be made into a splendid room. We had plans, when we first came, for turning it into a dark, William Morris-y antre similar in effect to that gloomy fantasy of a room in the Victoria and Albert Museum. Not that we would now – though you can still buy, quite readily and cheaply, those heavy papers and rich tapestry drapes that came into fashion seven or eight years ago. It would have begun by looking pretentious, and by now it would have grown tatty and depressing. A white ceiling, plain walls, and simple curtain fabric would do fine. Something clean and cheerful – without impinging, I mean.

After the children had stopped playing outside, I went to the window again. The martin was still at work, but I looked beyond it, beyond the garden wall, toward the view I've seldom stopped to contemplate. There are fields – one with tall hay soon to be cut, another with grazing cows – then a line of poplars and a market garden; a busy road then, and the farther meadows rising toward the South Downs. I can see a windmill that's celebrated in a poem by Belloc, and some marvellous stands of beeches where we sometimes go walking at weekends. It's a view to be grateful for, that I'm aware of, that I mention to new acquaintances when I'm asked about the place where I live. I turned away, though. The beauty would always be there to look at.

It would be there day after day at the window of this room. We're not likely to move from here. The view would be there week in, week out, the months making their slow accretions of years. To have reached middle age without having an illness more serious than childhood asthma is, I guess, unusual, and plain good fortune. Every morning that comes, I wake up in this room to thoughts of some incurable disease – cancer, diseased heart, or whatever – convinced that it can't be long before my luck runs out. Many people I've mentioned this to say they do the same. I get up, wash and shave, have breakfast, and set about the day's work; the morbid thoughts pass, only to return the following morning. I suppose this would be the room where I should be – I, or my wife, whoever was the first. Then the room would have to be taken note of. There would have to be flowers in that vase. The window would be spotless glass, to let in the endless skies, the breast feathers of the martin, the sweeps of Belloc's mill. You would listen in the room for whatever sounds would come to it: crockery on a tray being carried upstairs; the traffic on that road; after dark, intermittently, a restless bird under the eaves, twittering.

HISTORY OF A MAN IN 10½ BOTTLES

My grandmother had enormous forearms. You saw them best when she made pastry. Rolling up the sleeves of her black satin dress of a Saturday morning, she would begin, with gusto, to pummel flour, shortening and water to a bland submission.

This image of her on baking-day is my earliest memory. My grandmother was cosily (but not grossly) fat, and she wore a knitting needle to pin the grey bun of her hair. There was a smell of lavender wherever she walked. Apples she loved best – apples and cheese. You'd see her in the sun parlour, cutting a segment of Laxton or a slice of cheddar with a tiny silver dessert knife shaped like a scimitar. She would offer you some of her snack, and you'd feel the cool blade against your lips for that split second before your tongue explored the curious angularity of the tit-bit.

She lived to a great age. When we buried her (it was the one day of snow we had that winter) I remembered how I used to look up at those huge arms of hers as she rolled out the lids and linings of her pies. From elbow to wrist she was covered with the pink-white scales of eczema.

I shuddered a little at the thought as I stood at the graveside; shreds of beginning snow were falling on the coffin lid and would not melt.

47

I had not shuddered when I was a child. Her arms then had seemed strong, beautiful and protective, the colour and texture of breakwaters smothered with barnacles.

My grandmother did not own a wooden rolling pin. She used a pint beer bottle of the palest green. Sometimes it held a single flower – a rose, a moon daisy – in the sunlight at her kitchen window. There were letters embossed around the shoulder of the bottle. I suppose I began to learn my letters from her golden pies as she lifted them steaming from the oven. They always bore the imprinted message (but in mirror-writing, of course) ANSELL's BREWERY, BIR-MINGHAM: which you could read quite clearly when she held you, holding the cooled pie, aloft in front of her looking-glass.

*

Halfway along the brown-tiled corridor of my primary school there was a tall, glass-fronted cabinet. It was the school's museum. On its two visible shelves was arranged a congeries of unremarkable items, each with a handwritten label in Gothic, handsome script. I recall a fossil shell in a lump of chalk, a whale's tooth, an eightenth-century powder flask, and a dusty handful of Roman potsherds.

One day Lois Jones, the dark-eyed, curly-haired object of my first hopeless love, brought into class a piece of faded brown material, much perforated. Our teacher, Mrs Ash, feigned delight with Lois but was clearly dubious about the authenticity of the piece of rag. However, after three days (during which Lois devastatingly sulked and pouted in the cloakroom), the unpromising exhibit was placed in the cabinet between the fossil and the whale's tooth. The label read,

'Possibly a remnant of a lace dress which may have belonged to Emma, Lady Hamilton.'

Lois's radiance hurt me like a cramp that would not subside. I could not speak to her, for her beauty was insuperable. Those days, aged ten, you spoke only to plain girls in pigtails, and only then if they were not alone.

I ransacked the house for something interesting and genuine to present to the school museum. There was nothing. The only object we had worth considering was a mug bearing the portraits of Queen Victoria and Prince Albert. And I couldn't have that, my father said, because he kept his shirt studs and cuff links in it.

Bobby Baker, who sat in the next desk to Lois, presented a churchwarden pipe, the bowl of which was shaped like a skull. I was in despair.

My father, sensing my distress, said he'd try to find something for me at the shipyard. During the war he was a shipwright, helping to build and repair small vessels like gunboats and landing craft. He brought home a marlinspike. I liked the name, but it wouldn't do. He brought home a length of cordage, one end of which had been tied into an amazing knot called a monkey's fist; getting warmer, I said, but it wasn't up to, say, a powder flask. However, the evening he poured some ordinary-looking – but special – sand into a glass phial, I knew I had a winner. The little bottle of sand was given a prominent place in the museum; the Roman potsherds were moved an inch or two to make room for it. The imposing label (which partially obscured Lady Hamilton's purported lace) bore the legend, 'Sand from a Normandy beach scraped from the bows of a motor launch involved in the gallant action at Dunkirk.'

I happen to know that the exhibit is still on show, all

these years since. Lois Jones, I happen to know, married an unpleasant greengrocer thirty years her senior.

Wendy Upton was the first girl I ever kissed. She was the class monitor, a laughing, auburn girl who changed her name and the colour of her hair when she grew up and became a famous, and glamorous, TV actress; but it's Lois I think of whenever I see Wendy in a soap opera or some ad for frozen peas. If it had been Lois who had kissed me under the railway bridge that rainy afternoon after school, I would have poured the sand into the river and floated the little bottle away.

*

It was during my mid-teens that I bought my first bottle of champagne. To be strictly accurate, it was a half-bottle. The word BRUT on its label betokened the kind of aggressive masculinity with which I tempered an ever-growing aspiration to refinement and the Good Life. Once out of the *cave* in Rheims, and still blinking at the fierce sunshine, I attached the bottle behind the saddle of my bicycle. (I used the square-lashing technique I had learned in the Boy Scouts. You must begin, and complete, the lashing with a clove hitch.)

The year was 1949. With ten other boys my age I was on a cycling tour organised by the geography master. France still bore her war scars, but, unlike England, did not ration her food. We ate prodigious quantities of eggs and meat. In a street market I bought a honeydew melon, the first I had ever seen; I ate it standing astride my bike on a road overlooking an enormous war cemetery. Like the champagne, the sweet and exotic fruit was an assault on the pervading sense of austerity we'd left behind in England.

We rode about forty miles a day. Much of the time we

bumped across what were still cobbled roads. French bikes were specially adapted for such rough treatment, being fitted with ample pink balloon tyres and well-sprung saddles which cushioned both rider and machine against the implacable rigours of the *pavé*. At night, having pitched camp, we would do our best to repair the ravages of the day. Though our cycles bore heroic names – Raleigh, Hercules – they weren't up to the job. Nuts and bolts loosened; small, nameless pieces fell away; metal fatigue set in and the frames fractured. Mornings, early, we pressed on: through the Meuse valley, into Luxembourg, up and over the Ardennes, across flat Belgium, and so to Dunkirk, where we took the cross-Channel ferry.

At Dover, despite the clumsy handling of the crate full of our bikes as it was lifted out of the ship's hold, my precious half-bottle was still intact. On smooth English roads I raced the eighty miles home. I felt full of traveller's sophistication; had become a man of the world. My parents had never set foot outside England.

The moment I closed the door behind me, I called for three glasses. My mother and father (who had seldom lapsed since signing the pledge during World War I) watched with concern as I removed the wire, thumbed loose the cork.

All but a dessert-spoonful of the explosive wine gushed on to the living room carpet. I poured the dregs deliberately into the hissing foam on the floor, tossed the bottle, bouncing, on to the sofa. 'So that's that,' I said.

My father was appalled at the waste. He found the cork (it had lodged behind our elderly and dignified wireless set) and sniffed it.

He is a prudent man. Often, rubbing his chin, he will remark that my chronic extravagance began on that August afternoon in 1949. I acknowledge the truth of this. One of my favourite scenes in the theatre is the one in which Cyrano de Bergerac gives away a small fortune. '*Quelle sottise*,' says his friend. '*Oui*,' replies Cyrano, '*mais quel geste.*'

My father kept turpentine in that bottle. It lived in a cupboard in his well-ordered garden shed.

*

Robbo, the butler of my college at Cambridge, took a shine to me. One evening, after Hall, he offered to show me the wine cellars. We went through a trapdoor in the buttery. Robbo was – as always at that time of the evening – beamingly squiffy. I helped him down the precipitous, unrailed steps. He was in his uniform, full evening dress; I was in mine, polo-neck sweater, duffel coat, and academic gown.

In the remotest corner of the cellar, beyond the reach of the electric light, he lit a candle. By its flickering flame I saw a scattering of misshapen bottles covered with dust and cobwebs. Everywhere else in the vaults there were neat racks of port, sherry, claret, Burgundy and such, which Robbo ignored as we passed them. He stared reverentially at the mucky clutter at our feet.

'Not been disturbed since the day it was delivered,' he said. 'Genuine, original. Napoleon brandy. The Fellows open one bottle a year. Nobody else ever gets so much as a sniff of it. There's enough to last this century out.'

He allowed me to wipe the grime from one bottle with my cuff. It was distorted, the neck protruding at an odd angle and the heel thick and globular. Robbo snuffed the candle.

'I came here, age of thirteen, as a kitchen boy,' he said in the dark. 'I've worked my way up in life, been a good and faithful servant of the college. There's one more bottle here than the books show. I should know – I've counted them often enough.'

We mounted the stone steps. 'I retire next year,' Robbo told me as he closed and bolted the trapdoor. 'And do you know, in over half a century, I've never stolen so much as a Bath Oliver? You'd say that was worth a bottle of decent stuff, wouldn't you?'

I just grinned and thanked him. I wasn't going to push him toward, or pull him back from, his temptation. As it turned out, he died a month later from a heart attack. One of the Fellows I told this story to said that the brandy wasn't up to much, anyway. 'Got *too* old,' he said. 'Fifty years ago it was probably in its prime.'

*

It was the week before I got married. Between Cambridge and starting my career, I'd taken a temporary job as a semi-skilled labourer at Shoreham-by-Sea harbour. My job was to operate a steam hammer upside-down (the steam hammer, that is) extracting old steel piles from fifteen feet of mud. Because I had been to university, my mates assumed I was omniscient. Encouraged by this, from time to time I would let fall some esoteric trifle of information.

On a morning of relentless rain, the gang of us sat sheltering inside the canvas tea-shed quaintly known as a *tambu*. 'An Indian word, *tambu*,' I told them. 'Almost certainly brought home by British soldiers who served at the North-West Frontier.'

The gang whistled and sighed their amazement – all of

53

them except the scar-faced young Glaswegian sitting next to me. His name was MacKintosh, and he'd not long been released from Wormwood Scrubs.

'Originally,' I said to him quietly, 'your name would have been pronounced Mac*Kin*tosh.'

'It's *Mac*Kintosh,' he growled, tearing a hefty crust from his sandwich and throwing it with undue violence to the gulls swooping outside.

'Yes,' I said. 'All I'm saying is that once upon a time the stress would have fallen on the second syllable. Mac, you see, in both Irish and Gaelic, meant "son." Your forefathers' name, if you go back far enough, was *In*tosh.'

'My father was a bastard. He cleared out when I was a wee bairn. And he wasna Irish. He was a Jock through and through. His name was *Mac*Intosh. *My* name is *Mac*Kintosh. Shut ye fat face.'

'Listen,' I said, 'all I mean is –'

But MacKintosh had seized his tea-bottle by the neck, smashed it against the bench and was now shaking the jagged spikes within millimetres of my eyes.

It was to be a white wedding, Saturday at two o'clock in St Mary's. In silence I left the *tambu*, collected my cards and money at the site office.

That same evening I took a three-day job as barman, potman and cellarman in a local pub desperately short of help. My boss's name was MacIlroy. He taught me the jargon of the publican's trade, relishing arcane words like 'spilth,' 'ullage' and 'stollage.' 'Let me tell ye, laddie,' he said as he settled up with me on the eve of my wedding. 'Knowledge is power. Aye. Dinna forget that.'

*

The first winter of our marriage I went down with a bad case of penicillin allergy. I was covered all over with itching weals. I couldn't walk. I lay in bed, dabbing myself with calomine lotion.

The old Welsh crone in the next-door flat heard of my indisposition. She brought round a Winchester bottle about a quarter full of a remedy she said her family had been using for generations. All you needed to take, she said, was a teaspoonful: that's why it had lasted so long.

'It won't cure me, Mrs Williams,' I said. 'What I've got didn't even exist before they discovered penicillin.'

'It cures anything,' she said. 'Look at me, now, hale and hearty at eighty-two.'

I lacked her faith. Another four days I suffered the intolerable itching until it cleared itself up. The bottle remained on my bedside table, unopened. There was an advertisement stuck to it. I learned the copy by heart and often recite it as an example of a 'found poem.'

Sold by T. Jenkins, Swansea. CURIOUS AND INTER-ESTING. Price 3s. in one volume, octavo, of near 300 pages with an elegant portrait of the Author S. Solomon, MD.

A GUIDE TO HEALTH; or ADVICE to both sexes in a variety of complaints; explaining the most simple and efficacious remedies for those diseases which are treated on under the following heads viz:

Abortion / Address to the fair sex / Advice to nervous patients / Air / Appetite / Barren women / Bashfulness / Bathing, observations on, / Birth, particulars pertaining to / Body, unfavourable posture of / Bowels / Chlorosis or green sickness / Child-bearing / Chancres / Clap / Cold / Consumption / Conception / Cure for nervous diseases / Dancing / Daily exercise / Dejection / Deficiency of natural strength / Difference between venereal symptoms and those often mistaken for them / Digestion / Dreams / Exercise / Female complaints / Fits / Flannel / Flatulence or windy complaints / Girls / Gonorrhea / Gout / Gouty spasms in the stomach / Great schools / Heavy suppers / Hereditary diseases / Heartburn / Hypochondriac complaints / Hysteric affections / Immoderate evacuation / Internal sinking / Incubus or nightmare / Irregularity about the turn of life / Leprosy / Limewater / Lowness of spirits / Love / Maids of weakly constitution / Man / Menses / Memory, loss or defect of / Mothers, their duty / Nerves, weak / Obscene conversations, baneful effects of / Phthisis / Pregnancy / Quick digestion / Rheumatism / Riding on horseback / Rising early / Scurvy / Scrofula / Swoonings / Symptom of pregnancy / Tea / Temperance / Timidity / Ulcer in the throat / Venery – excessive / Venery – secret / Virgins / Voyages by sea / Walking / Water / Weakness / Wind / Windy liquors / Women's milk / Women / Youth

To the public

Every person young and old should purchase this book, there being scarcely an individual who is not interested in some part of it. In particular it is recommended to young men and boys; as an early attention to the latter may save to guard them from a fatal rock on which thousands have split and be the means of preserving their bodies from disease, and also their souls, their minds, and all their faculties from destruction.

They simply don't write bottles like that any more.

*

I was once privileged to meet, in a Swansea pub, the celebrated Welsh composer Dr Daniel Jones. He was in his
cups and so was I. Knowing in advance that we were to be
introduced, I was determined to write down in my notebook,
verbatim, the first remark he made on the subject of music,
What he said was, 'If you're ever without a tuning fork,
remember that a Guinness bottle, blown into, pitches a perfect cello *A*.'

*

A friend of mine, an American poet, collects beach glass.
On seaside vacations he gets up at dawn to look for it –
delicate little ovals of pastel-coloured glass. His collection is
exquisite. One evening, in his Greenwich Village apartment,
he tipped more than a thousand pieces of it from a velvet
bag on to the table; each one was lovely and individual as a
semi-precious stone you would pay good money for in one
of those rock shops. God knows how many tides and gales
of the Atlantic it had taken to smoothen and polish those
bits of broken bottles to such perfection. Would it take a
year of the ocean's scouring? A decade? Half a lifetime?

I said I thought this an original and satisfying hobby,
collecting beach glass; healthy, too, poking about the shore-
line at first light, breathing all that fresh air. My friend gave
me a piece to keep, a rare item, deep carmine red.

'I should have started when I was younger,' he said. 'Fifty
is no age for starting something new. And Nature is so

grudging and slow. But there are solutions to every problem. Come and look at this.'

He took me into his kitchen. He had one of those pebble tumblers at work, churning round and round endlessly with a grating sound. 'In there,' he said, 'is a Dutch beer bottle sent to me by a friend in Amsterdam. The green is the green of ripe olives. A week's tumbling in coarse sand, a week in medium, a week in fine. Then a day or two of jeweller's rouge, and the job is done.'

He showed me next the little hammer with which he smashes his bottles. I must have looked shocked; certainly the romance of his hobby had evaporated.

'It's a way of cheating Time,' he said. 'Like writing poems.'

*

My friend Dougan, with whom I was staying recently, took me to a wine tasting organised by his village society. On the way, I protested that I couldn't tell the difference between Imperial Tokay and Lundy Island Oloroso. 'It scarcely matters,' said Dougan. 'The great thing at wine tastings is to appraise the people, not the wines. You'll notice that sweet people find most wines sharp, the bombastic so-and-so's call every glassful humble, and the pretentious label everything as *un*pretentious. While they're all prattling on, you and I will have a good old guzzle.'

The event took place in the village hall. There were about a hundred assorted villagers present, most of them City types and their twin-set-and-pearls wives. Long tables, decently dressed with plain white cloths, bore the weight of many bottles; I calculated that there was enough wine open for everyone to have, say, five glasses. There were some good cheeses, each with a little flag bearing its name.

Above the desultory hubbub which, when we entered, had sounded like an interminable statement of sadness in the dusty hall, there soon rose a piercing whine of a voice neither male nor female. Dougan, his mouth full of Irish cheddar, knocked back some red stuff he'd poured from a randomly chosen bottle. 'Horrible,' he said; but before he could elaborate upon this verdict, the androgynous and querulous whining had begun again. It had the effect of subduing all other chatterers. 'The lower slopes, of course,' it was saying, 'and almost certainly *premier cru* and bottled in this country under licence. What one looks for, and is entitled to expect even of a fresh young wine of this sort, is total integrity – ah, what Henry James, had he been talking about wines, which, ha-ha, he was not, might have found the oenological equivalent of the, ah, "sky-blue soul."'

'The vicar,' whispered Dougan, starting on a hunk of Stilton.

'Reminds me of that Thurber cartoon,' I whispered back.

'"Naive and domestic Burgundy" etcetera. Right. He's like this every year. But he's going to get his comeuppance tonight.'

'Oh?'

Dougan told me how, the previous year, he'd invited the vicar to taste, and comment on, a wine which he, Dougan, had picked up from a shipper's in Town. It had been towards the end of the evening; a small crowd had gathered while the vicar sniffed, twirled, tasted, spat, and finally swallowed gulps from the anonymous bottle. Usually it was the vicar himself who chose the wines for the tasting; he was in cahoots, said Dougan, with Harcourt, the village wine merchant who charged fancy prices for indifferent plonk. The vicar ('Not quite an absolute fool, but almost,' Dougan said) had been unwilling to give the wine a name. Instead, he'd gone through the entire thesaurus of wine taster's jargon, describing the wine in extravagantly outlandish terms. 'It has been well rounded,' he had said in conclusion, 'the way a good carpenter such as Our Lord will chamfer off and sand down any sharp, not to say jagged edge.' Dougan would not tell him what the wine was. The vicar maintained that he'd never tasted anything even closely resembling it. It rang no bells for him.

'So I said I'd tell him a year hence,' Dougan said.

Several glasses and a wedge of Caerphilly later, the whine became a bay and I saw the vicar walking from his end of the hall towards us. 'My *dear* Mr Dougan, so *there* you are! I think you've been hiding from me.'

Dougan introduced us. The vicar's hand felt as if it had always been cold.

'Mr Dougan has been teasing me for a whole twelvemonth,' said the vicar, partly to me and partly to the group forming itself around us. 'I wonder, sir, if you will now vouchsafe to us what that tantalising beverage was with which you so mystified last year's little gathering?'

Dougan took a sealed envelope from his breast pocket. 'Read it at home, vicar,' he said, 'before you say your prayers.'

And then, abruptly, we left.

'Well,' I said in the car, 'what did it say?'

'Two things,' said Dougan. 'Hopkinson's Altar wine,' and a quotation from the Sermon on the Mount.'

'Which was?'

'"Judge not, lest ye be judged."'

*

I am, of course, stockpiling sleeping tablets. A man approaching his sixtieth birthday, who has lived as unwisely as I have, would be crazy not to. One's GP is wonderfully accommodating. When asked by my best friend what I'd like for a birthday present, I said, 'A half bottle of single malt, to keep by me.'

*

But in the meantime a man can grow very thirsty, telling stories. So now, if you will excuse me, I have, on ice . . .

THE BOW

Paul and I were alone in the house and would be the rest of the day. It was August, midmorning, prickly hot. The forecast had promised cooler weather moving across southern England from Cornwall, but the week-long heat showed no sign of relenting. After breakfast, I had watched from the kitchen window as Jean and the girls ran to the corner for the waiting bus. They were going to buy shoes. They were going to be in Portsmouth *all day* buying shoes. The bus had moved off and the tar on the road gleamed white. In the living room since then, I had been lying on the sofa; my cigarette smoke surged up into a shaft of sunlight and swirled, and slowly thinned, leaving dust. Paul played with his model cars in the far corner of the room, quietly. I would not speak until he did, and he would not speak. I worried about him. He was eight. He often seemed even more withdrawn at home than he was at school. Usually he was the one who was taken shopping, while I looked after the girls; we would fill the time cutting pictures from magazines or making wigwams from blankets and brooms: I could always be comfortable with my daughters.

I lit another cigarette and thought of Patsy and Monica walking through the department store later on in their new shoes. They would have to pass through the carpet depart-ment – that close, wadded area of quietness where sometimes in the winter months I would loiter for the sake of its warmth. Nobody would buy a carpet on a day like this, not if it meant standing about among the rugs and foam and underfelt and breathing that still air full of woollen particles. Jean would lead them through to the kitchenware, and they would naughtily clatter the saucepans for the cool relief of sound. And the three of them would run, perhaps, the length of the tiled floor. The new shoes would sound like rain. I sat up and looked at Paul over the sofa back. He was guiding his new Ferrari into an impromptu garage of books, his face pressed hard into a cushion. Eleven-thirty. I lay back to face the other way. I had to keep awake. Another five hours of this, I thought.

My neighbour was in his garden, playing with his twin boys. He was a man who would sometimes lose his temper with his kids, and I would watch his anger break, a spon-taneous harm amid his mindless, quotidian love. Soon – for I knew his rhythms – he would shout at one of them and go indoors for a drink, and the twins would begin some other game. After half an hour, he would be outside again when Marion came with the laundry basket to take in the washing, and he would make her wait while he put the boys in the laundry basket and pulled them three times round the cherry tree. Marion would stand there with her arms piled high with shirts, her shoulders draped with tights and hand-kerchieves, her knuckles white round a great clutch of pegs. She didn't mind his short storms of anger.

I got up and emptied the ashtray. I swept up the crumbs under the breakfast table. Paul raised his legs, without being asked, without looking, so that I could sweep round him.

There were crumbs sticking to his knees and his shirt.

'Stand up, Paul. I want to brush the crumbs off you.'

He stood up and let me do it. I went into the garden and scattered the crumbs for the birds. A helicopter was passing over low – a red helicopter that hurt every summer day with its slicing whine as it stood by for air-sea rescue. I wished that Paul would want to go down to the beach, but I knew he hated it when the tide was high. When he was four, he had run behind me once as I ran down the shelving beach; I hadn't heard him, and he had nearly drowned. At low tide, he liked to sit under a breakwater and listen to the sand flies in the weed, or dig a hole and sit in it and pretend he was sitting in a car. He wouldn't go – he'd have heard the helicopter and would know the tide was in. The twins were waving at the helicopter crew. One of them pretended to shoot at them with a bamboo cane. In the air, left empty when the helicopter had passed beyond the hazelwood and down out of sight to the dunes and whipped water, there was only heat and a soft, malignant shudder.

I went indoors. 'Paul,' I said, and was prepared to be patient, 'let's go somewhere to be cool.'

'I want to play with my cars.'

'You could bring them with you. Well, two or three of them. It's so hot in here, and Mummy won't be home for a long time yet.'

'I'm not hot. The helicopter just went over.'

'I don't mean the beach. Somewhere else. In the hazelwood, by the pond. It's nice in there. Shady.'

'I want to play with *all* my cars. I sting my legs on the nettles. There's a wasp nest.'

He was right. I thought of several other places, but I didn't mention them, because I thought straight away of his objections to them all. He crashed a grey Ford into a group of other cars, his face a mime of fire and violent death. I'd have to be patient. Then I knew what to do. 'How'd you like a ride on the motorbike?'

He'd never ridden on it before; Jean said he was still too young. He used to get on it in the garage, turning the throttle, making revving noises. His feet didn't quite reach the footrests, so he used to lie along the saddle, his toes in the luggage rack. That was months ago. Jean had stopped his going into the garage when he'd broken a bottle of paraffin.

'Mummy said I can't. My legs aren't long enough.'

'You've grown since then. Anyway, I can put blocks on the footrests. I'll shorten the strap on Mummy's helmet for you. You'd like that.'

But I could see he didn't like the idea at all. Jean's quiet talking to him when he broke the paraffin bottle had made him as frightened of the motorbike, and fire, as he was of the sea, and drowning. All the time, in his play, the drivers of his cars died in flames or toppled over a cliff of books into deep white water. One day, I'd come home and found him suspending a teddy bear by his pyjama cord. Jean had been amazed when I asked her if she'd warned him against putting the clothesline round his neck; no, she'd said, not the clothesline – the telephone cord. His play was his fear, but in his fantasies danger could not hurt him.

'We'll go to the top of Kingley Vale. I'll cut you a bow from the yew trees up there. And arrows.'

'I've got a bow. Look.' He ran across the room to his toy cupboard and took out one of those miniature pink plastic bows they used to give away in the supermarket with the detergent packets.

65

I smiled. 'No, I mean a real bow. Like Robin Hood. He always made his from yew wood.'

'It *is* a real bow. It works. I've got an arrow, too. Watch.' He had a crooked twig that he'd found in the garden. He pulled back the string as far as it would go, then released it. The arrow fell at his feet. 'See?'

'Lovely, Paul. But I mean a *proper* bow, taller than you. And some nice straight arrows. We'll cut the bow and trim off the side shoots and skin off the bark and notch the ends. Then I'll get some of that orange-coloured nylon line I bought for the runner beans to grow up. That'll make a good, strong bow. I don't know what sort of wood you're supposed to have for arrows. Some of those straight bits of dogwood in the hedge might do. Nice red arrows. Mummy can make you a quiver to carry them in. She's still got some of that rexine.'

'Can we go on the bus?'

'Don't worry about the motorbike. It won't catch fire while *I'm* there, will it now?' He almost smiled. 'You can bring as many cars as you like. They'll go in the saddlebags.' I'd won him over. 'And we'll take some sandwiches and lemonade, and we'll not come home till nearly bedtime.'

In less than half an hour, we reached the foot of Kingley Vale. Paul had clung very tightly round my waist all the way, and after I had stopped I had to unclench his fingers before I could get off and lift him down. He was pale and slightly trembling. I put the bike on its stand and took the food satchel from the saddlebag. He had only brought one car, which he'd put in his breast pocket. It was a police car, bristling with sharp radio aerials, but I wouldn't let myself say that it would be dangerous there, if he fell. I unstrapped his helmet and mine, and put them both in the saddlebags. I noticed how one of the footrest blocks that I had fixed had begun to work loose; and I shuddered, remembering the time when as a small boy I had caught my foot in my father's wheel and the ointment with a smell like candles had taken five weeks to heal the wound. The ridge of scar never got dirty, even when I walked miles along dusty lanes like the one up Kingley Vale. 'Run on, then, and try not to fall over,' I said. But I expected him to, for he was clumsy on his feet. And he was still trembling.

In front of us, the chalk path heaved, grasshopper-hot. Paul ran ahead, brushing aside high grasses and the slender lower limbs of a wayfaring tree. When he was fifty yards in front of me up the steep white scar of chalk, his ankles were in a pool of shimmer and the black flints that lay along the path seemed to move like dolphins in surf. He would be short of breath and sweltering in the cardigan I had made him wear, and I expected him to sit and wait for me under the holly bush just beyond him. In the hedgerow, chicory grew tall and ragged. On the way back, I'd pick some, and cornflowers and toadflax, to take home for Jean. While the girls arranged them in vases, they'd tell me about their shopping day; and Monica, telling me about her shoes, would do imitations of the shop assistant. It would be evening then, and cool, and after Paul had gone to bed I would go carp-fishing until after dark.

'Come on then, Paul. Not far now. You did run fast. There's the wood, look, all those dark old trees. From the top of the hill you can see the cathedral, and Bosham, and over the harbour as far as Portsmouth, where the girls are.'

'And Mummy.'

'Yes, of course, and Mummy.'

But when we reached the top and turned toward the sea, we were disappointed. A sea-fret lay across the town and the water, and we could make out nothing beyond the greenhouses at the bottom of the hill. A few yards inside the wood it was very cool and dark where we sat, and Paul shivered and took his toy car from his pocket and ran it along his leg. Near us was a piece of dead crow, half hidden in the silt of fallen needles. I thought of the druids under us, centuries deep, their ceremonies among the trees. On a hill not far away, I'd once dug up the bones of a Bronze Age man. I'd walked down the hill with his bones in a bag and his skull under my arm. I'd tell Paul about that one day, I thought; and about how I'd joined those bones together with bits of wire and hung him in a cupboard. He wasn't ready yet, though, for stories like that; or for knowing how my man's cranium had been stove in. There was no need to add to the boy's nightmares about violence and bloodshed and death. I wondered then, guiltily, how I'd justify to Jean the cutting of a bow and arrows. We didn't encourage him to play with toy guns. I looked around me. It was as quiet as could be in the wood. Until historically recent times, Man had always lived on these hills. What they'd died of most often, if not from fighting, was broken legs: they would fall, and be unable to hunt, and be left to starve. Today, Paul and I were utterly alone there, with the mist between us and the town. It seemed curiously remote and soundless, and the dust among the fluted old trunks made the nearer trees look like lunar stumps. There were no flies around the dead crow, no birds in the upper branches that we could hear.

'Dead people look funny, don't they, Daddy?' Paul said. 'Do they?'

'Yes. You know King Canute?'

'Yes.'

'His daughter was buried at Bosham. In the church. Mrs Scott told us.'

'That's interesting.'

'And you know what they did?'

'No.'

'They dug her up. And do you know what she looked like?'

'You tell me.'

'A pile of old cornflakes.'

He looked me straight in the eye, his hand over his mouth, waiting for me to laugh. When I did, he fell about giggling and rolled over and over down the slope of needles.

While I cut the bow, he played with the needles as he played with dry sand on the beach, piling them, letting them spill through his fingers. He kept laughing to himself, and when he looked toward me he made me laugh, too. I felt easy with him now – as easy as I was with Patsy and Monica. Cornflakes. Why not? Death needed to be like something you knew when you were eight.

The branch was cut. We dragged it to the edge of the wood into the sunlight. Out of the dark, the green waxy needles of the live branch seemed much longer. I hacked away the side shoots with my jack-knife and Paul threw the pieces back into the wood. He sat by my side as I peeled away the bark, and the damp stick shone in streaks of yellow and pink and then turned orange like a bitten apple. There was a far-off heaviness of percussive sound, almost like thunder. It was the noise that heavy books would make if dropped in a distant, carpeted room.

'What's that?' he asked me.

'Expect it's guns. The sailors are practising with their guns.'

'Where? What for?'

'Somewhere at sea near Portsmouth. They've got a gunnery school.'

'Mummy's at Portsmouth.'

'I know, but don't worry. They don't use real bullets. There, now, it's all peeled. Just let it dry a bit in the sun. Want a drink?'

I poured some lemonade in a beaker. He sipped it, looking towards where the sea lay concealed. The muffled thudding went on. I thought of Hardy's line, *It's gunnery practice out at sea* and the line that rhymes with it, *The world is as it used to be*.

'Daddy, when you were a soldier, did you kill anybody?'

'No, of course I didn't. I wasn't in a war. When the war was on, I was a little boy like you.'

'Well, why are there still sailors and soldiers and there isn't a war?'

'In case there's another one.'

'Will there be?'

'No.'

'Well, why –'

'When I was as old as you, I remember the planes fighting each other up there.' We were lying back now, looking up at the sky. It was the colour of the chicory flowers. The guns grew fainter. 'Sometimes I used to be playing in the fields with my friends, and we saw planes on fire come crashing down.' And I thought, I wasn't afraid then, during the Battle of Britain, as I would be now. Little boys had better things than World Wars to be frightened of.

'Daddy?'

'Yes?'

'Does everybody have to die?'

'Yes.'

'Oh.'

'Best be getting back now, Paul. Come on, you carry the bow and I'll carry the satchel. Remind me to pick some flowers when we get to the bottom of the hill.'

We walked toward the hole in the fence where the path began. There was still nobody to be seen. On the way down, I told him about Bronze Age men and Saxon warriors. As long as men had lived in England, they had fought each other for the hills where we were, I told him; but this hadn't happened for a long time, and it wouldn't happen again. Paul began to talk to me as he had seldom done before. I wondered whether he would always remember this day, this time, as I always would. He's nearer to forty than thirty now. I must ask him, next time he visits. I must ask him if he remembers saying he thought there would be no more battles, because nobody wanted the hills any more. I supposed, that day, as I still suppose, that he was right: the yew trees could grow and die in their own dark, and not many people would bother to walk from their cars up to them.

We picked the flowers and tied them together with a plait of grass. I tried not to let him see me weep, fretful about what might happen in his lifetime.

The girls were already in bed when we reached home. Jean said they were overtired and petulant and that she'd packed them off. We'd have to be careful with Monica, she said. She was getting wilful, a real little madam. All day she'd sulked, because she couldn't have the shoes she'd wanted. I listened as she told me about the crowds at the bus station and the noise of the guns and the prices of things. 'She'll be all right,' I said, 'you can worry too much about kids.'

Paul came and sat on my lap. 'Old cornflakes,' he whispered, and we both laughed, and I told my poor, distraught wife that I'd explain later.

THE HAIRCUT

Coming across an old photograph of myself, I was surprised to see that when I was still quite young I affected sideburns. There was a time, indeed, when I enjoyed going regularly to the hairdresser's. In the photograph I look reasonably confident, and happy, and presentable. A fellow like that might have made something more of his life, one might think.

I remember having it taken in one of those passport photograph booths, during one of my midweek trips into the city. It had become a regular job for me then, taking Dora Jones's little boy, Raymond, to have his hair cut. Every third Wednesday in the month we made our trip into the city, leaving the village where we lived on the early afternoon bus. I called for him at twenty past one, and we would walk to the bus stop by the clump of oaks opposite the post office. There, generally, we had four or five minutes to wait; we used the time listening to the rooks in the treetops, and I would tell Raymond a little poem I knew about the big black birds that called to one another the length and breadth of England.

One of those days I recall particularly well. I recited the poem over and over until we heard the bus straining up Gravitt Hill toward us. As usual, I carried Raymond to the back seat of the bus so that he could wave to his mother when we passed her standing at her cottage gate; as usual, he waved in her direction until he felt the swaying movement of the bus as it turned the sharp bend by Stimpson's Forge. This was the beginning of a ritual that neither Raymond nor I allowed to change. I always held him round the waist as he stood on the back seat, and I watched the way his huge-looking eyes rolled from left to right toward the blur his mother was in. An ugly contraption of wire and elastic held the glasses on his head; the thick, bluish lenses emphasised the pinkness about his eyes and the yellowish traces latent in his frightening white hair. Dora waved back, and smiled, as if he could see her. I felt that I should wave, too, but I kept my hands tightly round his waist in case he fell. Raymond was only three.

When Raymond's father had walked out on the two of them just over a year and a half before, the Parish Council Welfare Committee had met at once in order to decide what could be done for Dora and her sickly baby. I'd had nothing to do with any of the Parish Council members since my stand-up row with the chairman and treasurer about a sodium lamp they proposed to erect outside my cottage, which would look ugly and keep me awake at night. I knew they'd not come knocking at my door to ask for money or help. For the first six or eight weeks I contributed nothing to the communal effort, which, as I had expected, began to be half-hearted and sporadic. Other people in the village had their troubles and needed help; old Albert Smith had lost an arm at the sawmill on the very day it closed down, and the Hollands had had to destroy all their chickens after an outbreak of fowl pest. From what I'd heard in the post office, I gathered that Dora was thought to be over the worst of her troubles and that, since she was a strong young woman, she ought to be able to manage without further help. In any case, Social Security looked after those in need now, people were saying. And so, like the Hollands, who replaced their flock from a barely adequate insurance pay-out, Dora was released from the village's concern. After all, we weren't living in the old days any more, I heard it said.

It was soon after this that I began to trim the hedges round Dora's cottage whenever I did mine, and to tidy up the strip of flower garden each side of her front door. I took care never to go round to the back garden or to set foot inside her door, because I knew how many pairs of eyes were watching me from behind the curtains of Beulagh Terrace. Dora and Raymond helped gather up the hedge clippings and the weeds and burn them on the piece of waste ground between her cottage and mine; she would rake the fire while I held Raymond's hand and watched the smoke hang among the tall old trees at the roadside. The little boy was frail and almost blind, but he was very quick to talk. I supposed that this was because Dora talked to him all the time they were alone. Sometimes I stooped down so that he could tell me about his toys. He put his face very close to mine as he spoke, and ran his hands over my cheeks, and touched my glasses and the top of my head. As I listened and helped him with difficult words, I'd look over his shoulder at Dora stirring the bonfire. Guiltily, I used my close moments with Raymond to admire his mother's long, loose hair. It had the golden depth and lustre of brandy held up to the light; it was kept from tumbling round her eyes by a simple Alice band that crowned her head always, as the wire and elastic always crowned her son's. When Raymond ran his fingers through my hair, I imagined he was feeling for a band round my head; he would suppose that everybody had one. One evening, after he had tousled my hair and I had felt it thick and hot at my nape, I had suggested to Dora that I take him with me to the hairdresser's the next day. Dora was uncertain, for Raymond had rarely been out of her sight, but the outing had been a great success.

That day, then, for about the tenth time, I sat Raymond down after we passed the Forge and gave him the tickets to put in his purse. Then he turned toward me for the question he knew would begin our conversation.

'What will Mummy do while we're having our hair cut this afternoon?'

'She'll Hoover my carpet.'

'Is it a blue carpet?'

'No. Red one like my red purse.' Whether or not Raymond was colour-blind, we still don't know for certain. He probably was.

The line of Lombardy poplars went past, swishes in the hush outside. 'Cows in that field there,' he said.

'That's right, Raymond, clever boy. Cows.' The field was empty, and usually was, but there had been cows the first time we'd come past the trees.

'Big tractor in a minute.'

'What colour?'

'Red.'

We passed all the sounds that measured out the journey into the city. The electricity sub-station hummed while the bus stopped; a dog chained outside a filling-station yapped fussily. I closed my eyes to share Raymond's knowledge of the route, listening for rookeries, running water, Muzak from the country club, children's voices from a school yard, the thunder of our bus in the tunnel of the underpass, the clanking of wagons in the railway shunting depot, the first clamour of traffic at the feral edge of the city, the loudspeaker in the bus terminus at the end of our ride.

'Up you come, then,' I said, and he held me tightly as I carried him along the gangway of the bus, down the two steps and through the waiting room to the High Street.

For years now, I'd been spending my half days off in the city. When Sandra had left me, I had used to wander about the streets in the hope of seeing her in a shop or cafe. If I caught sight of a fair-haired woman dressed in blue – Sandra's favourite colour – even then I could feel a stir of excitement. There had been nowhere else for me to look for her except in the city where we had first met. Now that I was bringing Raymond with me, although I still had the habit of sauntering through the same department stores and drinking coffee in the same *espresso* bars, I was gradually losing the compulsion to examine the individual faces of a crowd. Watching over Raymond, teaching him how to drink through a straw, fastening the loose buckle on his shoe, picking up the toys he dropped and couldn't see was helping to diminish the arc of my concern. The city was becoming once more for me a comfortable, anonymous movement of people.

As we walked hand in hand through the throng that raggedly stretched into the vast central car park, I sensed the faces of the crowd flicking past, unindividual as the trees had been during the bus journey – men's faces, women's faces, all with the sameness as that line of trunks. For Raymond, half running, half walking, legs and flaps of coats would have seemed the same. We walked on within the little area that confined our dependence on one another and would admit no intruder; with our sense of each other centred in the hot clasp of our hands, we sidestepped running boys, accelerated past groping old ladies with push baskets. Through the Cathedral Close we put up flocks of pigeons that clattered like rain on iron roofs. Once we had scuttled through the slate-paved alley that echoed our footsteps high above us – poink, poink, poink – we reached the hairdresser's shop door, went through into the half-light and soapy smells, and heard the door sigh shut. The traffic noises outside and the cries of newsboys and market traders suddenly became muted and strangely artificial, like wild track to a radio play. In this place we were glad to be known, as we were not known on the other side of the door.

Bob had a customer in his chair, but when he saw Raymond and me he put down his scissors and comb and stooped facing us, with his arms outstretched. 'Come on, young Raymond,' he called. 'Let's see how fast you can run, then.'

I loosed his hand and watched him run across the waiting room to the three steps that led down into the inner shop. He found the handrail easily, and held it in both hands as he jumped, feet together, down each step; then he ran as fast as he could into the great white-coated expanse of Bob.

While Bob and Raymond twirled round and round the hair dryer in Bob's parody of a Viennese waltz, I took off my coat and hung it on a peg that I'd never noticed before. 'What's all this about, then, Bob? Real coat pegs?' I grinned at him as he was putting Raymond down. 'I used to feel a great affection for my own special nail. What've you done, Bob, cashed an insurance policy?' I picked up Raymond and sat him on a chair in the waiting room. When I looked again, Bob was back at work, shaving his customer's neck. Without turning to face me, he cleared his throat with an elaborate and exaggerated rattle – a mannerism Bob had developed over the years to introduce any portentous announcement, whatever the subject.

'Not only the pegs, if you don't mind, young Tom. What about the new bit of lettering outside above the door? Didn't you notice? And that new sign behind where Raymond's sitting. Fine thing if I pay out all that cash and my oldest customers don't notice. Holiday in Bermuda I could've had with the money I've spent out on this place the last week or two.' He held the hand mirror behind his customer – a young soldier, who grunted his approval of Bob's work without actually inspecting it. 'Nobody takes the trouble to use their eyes these days, and that's a fact,' said Bob, taking the strip of cotton wool from the soldier's collar.

I looked at the sign. It was an ordinary cardboard one, hanging by a cord from a picture hook; it had an arrow pointing toward the inner shop, and below the arrow the word 'SALON.' As far as I could remember, the sign that had used to hang there had been just the same, except, of course, that it had become stained with cigarette smoke over the years and dog-eared at the corners from being blown down on windy days. The soldier went out and Bob came and stood beside me as I stared hard at the sign, wondering what I ought to say about such an unremarkable object; having known Bob for twenty-nine of my thirty-one years, I guessed that he was testing me, as usual. 'Give up,' I said.

Bob went to the corner cupboard, where he kept his towels and razor cloths, and took out the old sign. He held it up beside the new one for me to compare them. The word on the old sign was 'SALOON.' 'Got to move with the times, you know.' He winked at Raymond and touched him on the shoulder. 'Things are looking up. Had a windfall. Thought

I might branch out a bit. Get an assistant, maybe, and another chair, phase myself out gradually. Go and have a dekko at the new shop front and tell me whether you like it. Come on, young man, let's get mowing behind those ears.' He lifted Raymond from the chair and started to lead him carefully down the steps.

I went outside and studied the new lettering. Where once it had said simply 'BOB'S,' in shaky, black roman capitals on a cream background, there was now the legend 'SALON ROBERT, COIFFEUR POUR MESSIEURS' in gold, knobbly letters such as I remember seeing on fairground vehicles, splendidly florid against a rich chocolate background. The red-and-white pole that had used to project above the door had disappeared. I felt first impressed, and tickled; then somehow disappointed and even betrayed. I went back inside. Raymond was on the high stool that Bob kept for small boys, and Bob was, with very great care, removing the boy's glasses; it was a difficult thing to do, without snagging a tuft of hair in the wire fastener.

'Very smart, Bob. Congratulations. Mind you, there's some of us who can remember when you called yourself a barber. I often think about that little old shack with the corrugated-iron roof that you used to have before the war. I couldn't have been much older than Raymond. My mother used to take me in my push chair. I was over that way the other week. Remember that long wall between your shop and St Michael's Hall? You can still just make out the letters of that slogan the Fascists painted on it.'

Bob turned toward me, but kept his hand on Raymond's head; this was his usual concession to a waiting customer's contribution to the conversation. 'That so?' he said. He still faced me, but drew the comb slowly through Raymond's soft, thin hair. He wouldn't continue his work until I developed the theme.

'You remember. There wasn't room enough for more than one person to wait. So if you were busy when we arrived, my mother used to walk me up and down by that wall, teaching me my letters. What a way to learn to read! "British Fascists Unite" was what it said. When it was my turn, you used to come out of the shop and call us. And you didn't have a special high stool for boys in those days. A cabbage box, with a nail that kept snagging in my sock when I swung my legs.'

'You were a proper little devil, Mister Tom. Never sat still. Not like young Raymond here.'

'You used to tell me stories while you were cutting my hair.'

'About Charlie Hungry.'

'A dwarf, wasn't he? Dressed in black.'

'With a magic paint-brush like the one I used for cleaning the clippers. A camel's-hair brush. Cost the earth, these days. Yeah. Charlie Hungry. Hungry days, they were, and all.'

'I've still got one of the first bits of writing I ever did. You ought to have it hanging up in here, like a diploma.'

'Why? What did it say?'

'Don't think I should tell you. Not now you're a *coiffeur*.'

He brushed a few hairs from Raymond's coat, smiling to himself. It was my turn. I sat in the chair, and while Bob shook the white cloth, twirled it in front of me, and tucked it into my collar I watched Raymond in the mirror. He would sit on the high stool next to me and say nothing until my hair was cut.

Bob pushed my head forward gently and began to run the clippers up my nape. 'I'll tell *you* what it said, then, Tom.

Something like "Bob Murray is a British Fascist and Charlie Hungry is his little friend." Never forget it. You wouldn't – a thing like that. You'd spelt it all correctly except for "little."

'That's right. L-i-t-t-e-l.'

'I said to your mother at the time, if you'd been seventeen years older, I could have sued you. Clever little bloke, you were. Used to feel sorry for you and your mother, the two of you living on your own. Wasn't so bad for you. Kids get over troubles easier than grown-ups can.' He nodded toward Raymond, then said to me, 'Don't suppose you can remember anything about your Dad, can you?'

'I only know what people have told me – how he used to swim out of sight.'

'Strongest swimmer I ever knew. He'd have swum the Channel, no bother. A man like him drowning. Cramp, we all reckoned.'

'He took stupid risks. A boy needs a father – not that I can say I ever suffered. It's Mum I feel sorry for. She should've got married again.'

The scissors touched my cheek, a momentary coldness. 'She could've done, you know,' Bob said. 'It wasn't for want of being asked.'

I hadn't known. Did Bob mean that *he* had asked my mother to marry him? I waited for him to go on, but as I watched him in the mirror, puckering his brow and setting his shoulders firm in a stance of concentration, I knew he would not. I felt stifled, astounded that he might have been my stepfather. *Old Bob*. A hair that had fallen over my eyebrow irritated me; I wanted to brush it away, but Bob held my head firmly as soon as I started to move. He put his head close to mine, on the side away from Raymond, and looked at me in the mirror and whispered, 'It's time *you* thought about something similar. Know what I mean? It's obvious you've properly taken to young Raymond, and from what you've said now and then, his mother's a good young woman. Do you want to finish up like me? What've I got to show after all these years? Nothing to speak of. Look at this shop. A lick of new paint above the door, a few fancy French words to make you laugh and keep the others guessing, and what does it amount to? At half past five I'll bolt the door and then there'll be nothing for me until I unbolt it at five to nine tomorrow morning. No comfort, no companionship. All my old friends dying off or moving away. Five years to go before I get my pension, and then I'll snuff it like they all do. And no kids to leave anything to. Don't you make my mistake. Not that it's any business of mine, of course, and if I'm poking my nose in where it's not wanted just forget everything I've said.'

Raymond started singing quietly, the little three-note tune in waltz time that he repeated endlessly when he was playing by himself. I watched him as he pushed his purse up and down his leg in time with his singing – *lah*-lah-lah, *lah*-lah-lah. When he was a little older, I thought, I'd take him to get a new pair of glasses; the frames of those he wore had become too small for him. Now that he had had his hair cut, I could see how the wire arms were biting into his skin. Bob pushed my head right down so that he could shave my neck. I saw on the floor in front of me the snippings of my hair and Raymond's, brown and white.

'Bob, I'm pretty sure you're right,' I said. 'And don't think the thought hasn't struck me before. Sandra's not likely to come back. Not now. It'll be six years this coming Easter since she went away. Not seen her, not had a word. It struck me on the way here today that I don't think about her very much any more. But it's not that easy, is it? Raymond's mother's a fine woman, very attractive, and a good, steady sort. Come to that, I think she mightn't be surprised if I asked her to –'

'Well, then. What you got to lose?'

'All that divorce business, for a start. I don't know how you go about it. Never had one in our family. My mother wouldn't –'

'Not for her to say. She should have spoken up before, when you were courting that Sandra. Now, if I'd been your father, I'd have –'

'You did. Bob. You did warn me. I can't say otherwise. You were right. But how do I know Dora would go through the courts? And suppose she turned me down? It'd be awkward then, wouldn't it? That'd be the finish. I'd not be able to go round and see the two of them, do their bit of garden. I'd be so embarrassed. Know what I mean? Wouldn't be able to bring young Raymond on his outing here.'

Bob took the cloth from me and shook it. I put my glasses back on.

'Tom, you know you love them both. Now, instead of taking young fella-me-lad for his tea when you leave here, just you catch the early bus back. When you get there, don't mess about humming and harring. Come straight to the point. Put it to her that it'd be the most sensible thing all round. Not before telling her how you feel, of course. No, put that money back in your pocket. Your haircut's free today – just as it was when you were a sprog like this 'un. That's something else you didn't know, isn't it? Buy a box of chocolates with it. Something nice.'

I tried to put the money in his till, but he put it in my

breast pocket. I took my coat from the new peg, put it on, and lifted Raymond when he came to me so that he could open the shop door, which he always did. Bob lit a cigarette and sat down in his chair and began to look at his newspaper. He wasn't going to say anything more.

'Thanks, Bob. I like your improvements.'

He didn't answer, just waved his hand.

Raymond opened the door and we were back in the relevant noise of the city. Breaking our usual routine, I carried him to the bus station along a different, shorter route than the one we were accustomed to take. I was going to do what Bob said; I'd always thought of him as a sort of surrogate father, repeating his opinions at work as if I'd thought of them. He was quite right, as always. Part of the way through the city centre I ran, clutching the boy tightly. I wasn't going to miss that early bus back.

The bus was beginning to move as I scrambled on. The conductor held my arm, helping me up the steps. I slumped, out of breath, into the nearest seat, instead of going to the back. I kept Raymond on my knee. I took the purse from his pocket, opened it, and took out the money for the fare. 'Give the man the money for the tickets, Raymond,' I said.

'My nose itch.' There was a piece of grey fluff in his nostril; I had been pressing his face closely against my woollen cardigan as I'd run for the bus. He'd remember that, perhaps, when he was grown up, I thought. He began to cry as I brushed away the fluff. 'No tea,' he said, in his sobs.

'Not today. We'll have some tea when we get home. Not long.'

He cried all the way back to the village. He'd never cried with me before. I should have given him his tea. I'd broken our ritual. Children shouldn't be disappointed like that. It

85

wasn't the tea he wanted – just going to have tea. He never ate much. He needed building up. I would see to that. We reached the village and got off the bus. The driver opened his window and threw a paper bag to me. 'Give it to the lad,' he said. 'Poor little sod.' There was half a bar of chocolate in the bag.

We walked hand in hand past the post office and the greengrocer's. I knew what I was going to say to Dora. She'd ask me in, as she always did, and she'd be surprised when I agreed, and she'd know there was something special in the air. Raymond had stopped crying. I sat him on a wall and broke a piece of chocolate and put it into his mouth.

'Come on, then, let's dry those tears away, shall we? Mustn't let Mummy think you've been crying, must we?' I took out my handkerchief and dabbed it on his cheeks and under his glasses. I kissed him on the head as I lifted him down.

We crossed the road by Beulagh Terrace, and Raymond opened the gate and ran up to the door. When I reached the door, I wiped the chocolate from his mouth and put my handkerchief away before I rang the bell. Raymond knocked on the door with the metal rim of his purse. We waited for a few seconds, and then I rang again. Usually, Dora opened the side window before I finished ringing, but there was no sound from the house. Raymond kept on knocking at the worn paint on the door. A flake or two fell.

I took Raymond's hand and walked with him round to the back door. The kitchen window was half open. I put my hand inside and lifted the catch, opened the window wide. I shouted in. 'Dora? We're back. Are you there?'

I didn't wait for an answer, but walked in by the back door. Raymond had found one of his toys on the step. I'd been in the cottage once before – years ago, in the years when it had lain empty. I knew that the smaller of the two doors leading from the kitchen gave access through a passageway to the front sitting room. As I opened it, I heard Dora call.

'That you, Tom?'

'Yes. Can I come in? I did knock, but you didn't hear me. Have you been having forty winks?'

I looked round the door-jamb into the sitting room. Dora was looking into the mirror. She had her back to me. She was standing so close to the mirror that she touched it once or twice with her knuckles as she combed her hair briskly. 'Wait out there a minute, Tom. I won't be long,' she shouted.

I enjoyed being there, watching her while she didn't know I was only a few feet away. I had used to watch Sandra sometimes, like that. She gathered her lovely hair into a rope behind her, and slipped the Alice band along it, and patted it into place on the top of her head. She took a pace back and tucked in her blouse. I knew that I loved her, and wanted to make love to her. When she turned round, and looked surprised at seeing me, I was smiling in readiness. 'Raymond's outside, on the back step,' was what I said.

I heard a tap being turned on upstairs.

'Oh, Tom, there you are,' Dora said. 'Now you're here, there's someone I've been wanting you to meet. Sit down. Would you like a cup of tea?'

UNDERGROUND

An August Saturday, mid-afternoon. Halfway across the Thames, a slow train up from the coast almost halts. Alfred Thomas, a commercial artist fat before his time, has slept through the South Downs, the Weald, the nondescript suburbs. Now he stirs, gazes upriver through dirt-pearled glass at the raft of traffic shimmering on Chelsea Bridge. London, a hateful city in summer weather, is heat-struck. The tide is dead low, water the colour of dregs of milky tea. Alfred observes a yellow balloon dipping and jinking above a small flotilla of gulls. The image might be useful to Alfred one day, but he is too weary to make a note of it. He stands, straightens his tie, reaches for his bag and for the umbrella that looks preposterous on such a day as this. The train creeps past a signal box, asphalt yards. Beside the track there are three men leaning on shovels. They stare sadly down into a fire the sunlight makes flameless. And now shade, the long platform of Victoria station sliding by. Sparrows fighting for a grey crust.

*

In the station hall, Alfred buys a *New Statesman*; also a plastic cup of British Rail coffee, which, once sipped, he abandons. He wonders how to kill ninety minutes before the rendezvous at Liverpool Street Station. It will take, say, half an hour at the outside to cross town. This leaves an hour or so – scarcely enough time to visit a gallery. The pubs are shut. There's nothing within walking distance of Victoria worth walking to see except Westminster Cathedral. Alfred shudders, remembering the actual corpse of a martyr in there, the skin silvered over. His lapsed Catholicism is like a library ticket long since expired which he cannot bring himself to throw away.

*

Taxis swarm like black flies on the station forecourt. Beyond, in their separate compound, stranded buses look distressed in their bright-red paint. Alfred takes the staircase down to the Underground, grateful for its neutral climate under artificial light. Liverpool Street is one of the stations on the endless loop of the Circle Line. Alfred could travel in either direction to reach it – eleven stops one way, sixteen the other. He will ride round and round under central London until the minutes have elapsed. He will decide, by the spin of a coin, which platform to depart from: heads clockwise, tails counter-clockwise. Heads it is. The curds of a week's anticipation sour in his belly. The smell of the Tube brings on a spasm of coughing. Alfred imagines the scent of lemons. It helps. When he was a small boy, Alfred used to carry a lemon to smell on the way to his hated school, past fish shops and filling stations whose smells made him retch.

*

He slumps in a seat, the doors slam shut, the manic scream of the tunnel begins. Alfred shares his carriage with a party of Japanese tourists, festooned and dismayed. In Tokyo, Alfred remembers, there are men employed to cram people into underground trains; how long before that happens here? He makes an inventory of the cities in which he has ridden underground: Glasgow, Paris, New York, Moscow, Barcelona. You can be anonymous down here, an unsung Orpheus. Only once – it was on the Lexington Avenue express – did Alfred ever see someone who looked like anyone he knew. It had been startling: what was his dead Latin master from St Paul's doing in Manhattan, dressed in garish clothes? Under the surface of the earth, one is entitled to meet only strangers.

*

Sloane Square. The Japanese get out. Either they're staying in one of those bleak hotels just off the square or they've come to look at boutiques in the King's Road. Alfred pictures his elderly aunt among the roses at the Chelsea Flower Show; the ragged hermit poet in his boathouse near the World's End; that pizza place where a neatly dressed man, no more than Alfred's age, died of a heart attack at an adjacent table. Slam.

*

Will she come? If she comes, what will she be wearing? Her eyes are the colour of the stone called tiger-eye. South Kensington: the Geological Museum, her eyes on display, under glass. Her skin, sallow, the colour of old white ivory, latently yellow. Will she die young?

*

Gloucester Road. On that platform (how long ago?), a foreign baroness was once murdered. Slam. Alfred watches the spot slip by. Gun, knife, some blunt instrument: Alfred cannot remember.

*

Thinks of his children. They will be on the beach; per-haps – perhaps not – thinking about him. Nancy, thirteen; Michael, eleven; Patrick, ten. All strong swimmers. So was Victor, his father's oldest friend, who drowned in shallow water. Every day, in case they die, Alfred kills his children in his mind. When will they begin (have they already begun?) to find him out in his lies? He is a bastard. Things can't go on like this; but they will. Above, in a store in High Street Kensington, Alfred bought coloured lights for Nancy's first Christmas tree. A bastard, yes, and, like most bastards, sentimental. Anyway, the beach is crowded, safe.

*

The new beer ad they're slapping up is as witty and original as anything Alfred has seen this year from the opposition. The perennial question: how to steal, adapt, make one's own? And suppose Julia were his – his to keep? She drinks white rum. Taking her into some smart bar is like sailing into

harbour on a brand-new yacht. Upstairs is The Hoop,
Notting Hill Gate, which (time was) used to be one of
the best new pubs in London. Alfred would settle, this
minute, for a plain pint – on his own, in the back bar. By
opening time, five-thirty, she in that long white dress,
showy as a spinnaker, he will be feeling better. A Bacardi,
straight; a Canadian Club *on the rocks*. Glamour, aha, because transatlantic: never mind that ice ruins whisky,
or that scotch is peerless. And she: 'Was it easy, getting
away?'

*

Yes, easy. It's the going back that is difficult; being jocular,
inventive, a repatriate genuinely glad to be home, kicking
off his shoes and saying, 'I want to stay in one place for
twenty-four hours: kiss me.' The hardest of all, receiving
Gloria's kiss, not flinching. Feeling guilt surely indicates
some thread of goodness; like rogue's yard in a naval rope,
it also betokens – inextricably woven as it is through Alfred's
life – that he cannot be stolen without risk of detection.
Bayswater – the very mention of the name still makes Alfred
feel unclean. The first week after he and Gloria had returned
from their honeymoon, it was this time of year. In Hyde
Park, that black whore had propositioned him as he walked
from work toward the Tube. 'Something to whisper to you,
sir,' she'd said, and he'd let her put her tongue deep into
his ear. Her name, too, was Gloria. Striding away, he'd
turned round and asked. 'Gloria,' she'd said, 'you stuck-up
white bastard.' In the damp flat in Golders Green, every
evening for a week Alfred bathed his ear with antiseptic.
Their bedroom smelled like a hospital ward. A sore spot on

his scalp, he told Gloria, that would soon clear up. 'Oh' was all Gloria, his Gloria, said.

*

Paddington, the terminus of the old Great Western Railway. Chocolate-and-cream carriages filled up with schoolchildren evacuees. Alfred was Alfie then, innocent, with a label bearing his name and address tied to his mackintosh buttonhole. The war itself was not frightening – not frightening like being sent away (an only child) with his gas mask and ration book to a place of orchards where the earth was a different colour. Alfie had stood amid tracer bullets and found them beautiful; found beautiful the stick of bombs falling elsewhere, exploding out of sight. It was the great gouts of steam creating a new weather in the glass hall of Paddington, the smell of other children, the guard's whistle, piercing as fingernails on glass and making that vast crater of separation – these were the real terrors of war.

Of which, of course, Julia knows nothing. Alfred is almost – but not quite – old enough to be her father. She is naive but not innocent, whereas Alfred at seventeen was innocent but not naive. What embarrasses him most about her is the way she gives objects proper names. 'I'm getting another Basil,' she will say, investigating her face in a hotel room. Basil is a pimple. She has a hairbrush called Angelina (or Angelica, is it?) and a hat called Donald. Yet she lost her virginity at twelve. She calls Alfred's belly Anna-Maria, enjoins him to call her breasts Peter and Paul. At her age, Alfred had read the complete works of Proust in the original. Edgware Road. Slam.

*

93

Not that he wants her for sex. She is inept, and Alfred is disinclined to teach her the finer points. He likes looking at her. Baker Street, only a step to Mme. Tussaud's. Make of her a waxwork. She would melt.

*

Melt, as in that horror film, the ivory flesh sliding from the maquette and only the tiger-eye eyes remaining. The eyes, yes, and maybe the hair, nonflammable. The hair is good — straight, ample, waist-length, chestnut or russet according to the way the light falls. The hair, then, and the eyes, to be kept in a drawer for reference. Slam.

*

The bone structure, frankly, is bad. The skull (Alfred once heard a child describe a skull as 'a smile made out of bone') needs all that hair to conceal its coarse shortcomings. Also, the hands and feet are brutal when examined in detail. She wears long dresses with ballooning sleeves, has been well advised.

*

Alfred yawns, yawns again, closes his eyes, folds his arms (still grasping the rolled *New Statesman*), dozes.

*

King's Cross.

*

Farringdon.

*

Barbican. Alfred's cheek is comfortable against cool glass.

*

Moorgate. Alfred's accountant is two streets away. Alfred is in trouble with his taxes. He has claimed hotel and meals expenses without producing receipts. The receipts, bearing names not his, amount to something approaching seven hundred pounds. Alfred has a place to hide such things. A place where Gloria wouldn't think of looking.

*

Liverpool Street. 'Meet me,' Alfred had said to Julia the Sunday before, 'next to my name near the ticket windows in Liverpool Street Station.' There is a War Memorial up there listing the railwaymen who died in two world wars. Alfred does not know for certain whether a namesake of his appears on the list, but it's an even bet. Thomas is common. Alfred was, a generation back. There would have been a whiskered porter who fell at Ypres. Alfred is adept at arranging witty, intriguing, or whimsical rendezvous. His affair before last, he met a certain Mrs Bebbington, a buyer for a large store in Oxford Street, in the crypt of

St Paul's Cathedral next to the Duke of Wellington's funeral carriage.

*

Aldgate.

*

Tower Hill. Alfred's shirt has pulled up, and his navel is visible to a small boy sitting opposite. It winks, like an eye, to the rhythm of Alfred's breathing.

*

Monument. Alfred is awakened by the small boy's shrill laughter. He adjusts his shirt, realises he has passed his stop. It will come round again. Liverpool Street is behind him, ahead of him. He checks his watch, then tries, but fails, to relax.

*

He has heartburn, knows how ridiculous he looks. His mouth is sour. Tomorrow morning, how will he disguise his bulk, crossing from the bed to the sink in whatever room in whatever hotel he might wake in, beside her? The trick is to have a thickly quilted dressing-gown. You slip it on while still under the covers, avoiding kissing until much use has been made of the toothbrush. That, too, is a problem: how to remove a denture, scrub and replace it, without its being seen? Run the water fast, hunching over.

Alfred could write, and illustrate, a manual called 'Savoir-Faire for Beginning Adulterers.' He sucks on a peppermint lozenge, clutches his umbrella for a token of dignity. The small boy, who has unmatched ears, gets out at Mansion House. Slam.

*

She has a brother the same age as that boy. The same age as Patrick. To be her father he would have had to marry at seventeen. Her age. Blackfriars.

*

What is it about her, then? Her beauty, unclothed, is cumbersome. Alfred prefers her dressed, standing up, in quarter profile, silent. Best, when he returns from the Gents' while she waits for him at the bar, prinking her hair. Or, seated, eating enormously from a great dish of curry. She reminds him of a minor figure in a minor Pre-Raphaelite painting. She is without humour. Subtlety is lost on her. She is without seriousness. If Alfred painted her, he would be inclined to make her grotesque. Her youth is not of advantage, except when he is aware of other people looking at them. Slam.

*

And what does she see in him? Certain things that, frankly, Gloria either does not see or affects not to see. Alfred, Alfred is bound to admit, is clever, successful, urbane. His designs are in demand in several countries, and his book on textile prints is a standard work. She never tickles him as Gloria often does. (Her little finger in his navel.)

*

Westminster. That promise, God, to bring the kids and Gloria to see the Houses of Parliament. Alfred solemnly swears to bring them before the summer is out. But the bombs, the Irish outrages? A risk, maybe, but small during the recess. (Gloria's long-fingernailed finger sharp in Alfred's imagined belly button: nice.) After the tour of Parliament, the Abbey; after the Abbey, a picnic in St James's Park.

*

It would be worth a try, another try, to regulate his life. Greed – for food, for women, for whatever – becomes a habit. Habits don't break too easily, though. Can Alfred lose a couple of stones by Christmas? Can Alfred cut down on women, too? One less, say, a year? Will Alfred kick off his shoes, be kissed without flinching, stay in his home for up to forty-eight hours? What is it that Alfred needs, Alfred asks himself. Not sex – different sex, that is; not youth; not excitement; not schemes; not love, beyond the love he feels entitled to. What Alfred needs is not to have to put his virility to the test. He has proved, beyond any possible doubt, his ability to pull any woman he choses. It has all become a time-consumung bore. All he needs right now is what he will settle for – a pint of flat (or, if necessary, gassy bottled) beer. There's usually a bar on the 17.02. Alfred will go home to Gloria and the kids.

*

The job was called off, Alfred will say. That damned photographer didn't turn up on time and Alfred was damned if he would wait another damned minute in the damned studio. Something like that. Meanwhile, the tide is rising under Chelsea Bridge and this evening, were Alfred to be there to see it, there might be an interesting effect of mist over the oily water. Frame, say, a lamp standard with *its* light, a yellow balloon with *its*. Let a girl be seen in quarter profile by the lamp, her arms stretched toward the loosened balloon. She will be in white – the off-white of mist. Blur the edges, use it to sell anything from sparkling wine to milk chocolate. You see girls like that everywhere. They spring like antelopes down Oxford Street, up for the day from Milton Keynes.

*

In the refreshment buffet, Alfred slaps down coins, gratefully sips insipid beer as the fast train to the south coast accelerates past Battersea power station. He would have to concoct some lie for Julia. Then another, then another, until she finally lets go. Though to be perfectly candid, Alfred confides to himself, he couldn't be certain she'd have turned up anyway.

THE PEACE ROSE

As I guessed he would, my father-in-law came outside to watch while I planted his rosebush this morning. He'd have heard the barrow rattling with tools as I wheeled it past his window, and I daresay he observed me taking out the first spadesful of earth while he put on his hat and coat and found his walking-stick. He's old and infirm, but nothing much escapes him. Aware that he was shuffling very slowly toward me over the drenched lawn, I thrust the spade into the ground and leaned on it, waiting for him. He caught my eye, grinned, and then began again to win each painful and unsteady step of the distance between us.

He'd been looking forward to this. Five weeks ago, at the beginning of October, he and my mother-in-law had moved down from London into the annexe of our house. I'd been busy since then. This was the first chance I'd had to attend to the rosebush he'd insisted on my digging up from his small, meticulous garden and bringing with the rest of their belongings. The Saturday they arrived, well after dark, I removed all the leaves from the bush, lightly pruned it, and heeled it temporarily into some moist compost in the shelter of the garden wall. If necessary, it could have stayed there until the spring; but on several occasions he'd asked obliquely when I thought I could get around to putting it into its permanent station. 'Fair planting weather,' he'd said, on a couple of consecutive evenings, as I garaged the car after work; and 'Early autumn's the favourite time for getting off to a good start,' he'd said yesterday, while I was clearing the leaves from their back path.

'The soil still looks warm from summer,' he said to me now. 'The roots can get a fair grip before that first bad frost sets in.'

He was right enough. A good fortnight before their move down here I'd prepared the new, trapezium-shaped bed, and I'd shifted into it two dozen or so of my own Queen Elizabeths, framing a generous space in the centre for this huge old Peace Rose of his. The Elizabeths had already settled in well, and some of them had even made a few new buds during the Indian summer.

'Are you going to be all right there?' I asked him, once he'd steadied himself against the laburnum tree. The muscles in his legs are wasting; after the effort of his walking so far unaided, I was afraid he might slip and fall. 'Take no notice of me,' he said. 'I'll just have a bit of a smoke and watch you get on with it.'

There had been a heavy shower since dawn. When he fumbled to light a cigarette, he jolted back against the trunk of the tree and a spray of raindrops spattered down on him. 'No, no – it's all right, I can manage,' he said, as I took a pace towards him; but he knew I'd seen the cigarette disintegrate through his arthritic fingers, and the shreds of tobacco and sodden paper falling between his feet. 'Too soon in the day, in any case,' he said. 'It'd only make me cough.' And so I nodded, took hold of the fork, and made a show of loosening the subsoil I'd already loosened at the bottom of the hole.

He can't bear to have anybody help him. What he needs, times like this, is a short spell on his own to get things done the way he knows how. If he has a minute or two, unflustered, he can perfectly well extract the tin from his jacket pocket and prise open the lid with the second joint of his forefinger; then, if there's nobody too close to see him do it, he can easily hold the tin to his lips, like a Chinaman with a rice-bowl, and flip up a cigarette it took him ten minutes to roll after breakfast. Over the years, on the sly, I've noticed these special skills of his developing. He has his own kind of high-tariff dexterity with his Zippo lighter, too. He'll cradle it in the palm of his right hand, snap back the top with a brusque movement of the left wrist, rub the wheel along the ball of his rigid left thumb. I reckon that if he could guarantee being left alone a long while in a well-lit room he could still find the means, through his unyielding hands and fingers, of repairing the most delicate watch. Had this been his garden, not mine, he'd have had the rosebush planted a month ago. It would have taken him the best part of a whole day, but he'd have completed the job – and well – bit by bit.

'You're making a right meal out of loosening up that bottom,' he said. 'But I know what it's like, trying to get something done with someone breathing down your neck. I'll go back indoors.'

'It's not that,' I said. 'I've just been thinking. I ought to make up some planting mixture to scatter round the roots. Should've done it before I got started. Won't be long.' And I strode away before he could argue about it. But he probably guessed that I'd dug in plenty of good compost when I'd got the bed ready and that I simply wanted to give him the opportunity of enjoying his first smoke of the day.

After mixing peat and bonemeal together in a pail, I looked
at him from the shed window. He was prodding the ground
with his stick, testing for firmness. His cigarette was lit by
now, and a ragged streamer of smoke was rising through the
bare twigs of the laburnum. He looked frail but obdurate, a
waif in some old-fashioned, sentimental movie. I was glad
to see him there. When the fine weather came round again,
he would become a familiar figure in my garden. He's into
his eighties; I wondered how many more years he had left
to enjoy it before he had to be confined to the house. I felt
fond of him, protective towards him. Maybe he ought to be
offered a plot of his own to look after, I thought – some
easily manageable, compact bed it would please him to tend.
He'd be able to push a light Dutch hoe between some vegetables, or keep the hose running during dry spells. These
days it's possible to buy all manner of tools and gadgets
specially adapted for the disabled. He'd be glad to feel he
was being useful. However, there were months to go before
any such idea could be entertained. First, he had what
promised to be a severe winter to get through; frost, snow
and ice couldn't be far away now. In March I'd take the
garden furniture outside again. He could sit at a table by
the laburnum tree while I pruned the roses. Probably he'd
try to cut back his Peace Rose himself. I hoped it would
flourish for him. I threw an extra handful of bonemeal into
the pail and stirred it in.

'That looks like a bit of good, rich stuff,' he said, when
I put down the pail in front of him. 'What are those white
flecks – hoof and horn?'

'Bonemeal,' I said. 'Hoof and horn's a thing of the past.'

'Hoof and horn. Bagged it up by the ton when I was
a kid. Of course, that's going back seventy years. Came

from the slaughterhouse into the crusher. Stank to high heaven.'

I dropped four or five double handfuls of the planting mixture into the hole and then raised it into a mound for the roots and stock of the bush to rest on.

'And Irish moss peat,' I said. 'Best there is.'

'All wrong, having to import stuff like that. Fancy having to buy it! Leaf mould, my Dad always swore by. Tie an orange box on the back of your bike, take the coal shovel with you out of the hearth, cycle up to the woods. Lovely, that mould. Soft as a woman's glove when you sank your hand in it. All those trees got felled, though, when they built the housing estates.'

'Which trees?'

'Beeches. Long time before you were born. All part of Greater London now. We did our courting up in those beechwoods. You'd say you were going to get leaf mould for your father's roses, but really you were going to have a few hours with your girl.'

I held the bush by the tallest stem, placed it on the mound, and kicked in enough loose soil to hold it in place. 'Think it's going to look all right here?' I asked him.

'My old man knew what I was up to. He never said anything, but I know he knew. He had his leaf mould, he was happy. Yes – the bush'll look fine as it is. Just needs treading in. It'll do. By God, though, that's turning cold all of a sudden.'

'We'll go inside for a cup of tea,' I said. 'I can finish this off later. Don't want you taking a chill.'

I persuaded him to place his right hand on my shoulder, so that I could steady him over the grass to our back door and into the kitchen. My wife was rolling out pastry. 'Your dad's pinched with cold,' I said to her. 'Put the kettle on, will you?'

Jane filled the kettle and plugged it in as we sat down. 'Your mum might fancy a cup, too,' I said. 'Shall I go and fetch her round?'

My father-in-law shook his head. 'I shouldn't bother, if I were you,' he said.

'It's no trouble.'

'A fool's errand,' he said. 'She's probably not out of bed yet.'

'But it's gone eleven,' said Jane. 'Not like her.'

'Well, it is Sunday, after all,' I said. 'She's having a lie-in. And why not?'

'It isn't that,' he said. 'She never gets up at the right time these days. If I didn't keep on at her, she'd stay put until the afternoon.'

'I don't like the sound of that,' said Jane. 'Something's the matter. Maybe she ought to see the doctor.'

'No. There's nothing untoward the matter with her. Only the sulks and general cussedness. I don't know what anybody can do about it. She didn't want to move down here, and staying in bed is her way of paying me out. I expect she'll get used to it. Just got to come to terms. Take no notice.'

Jane sighed. 'It's so silly,' she said. 'You're so much better off here. Country air. Out of that damp old house which was falling down round your ears. Away from all that noise and dirt, the planes taking off and landing every few seconds at Heathrow.'

'You don't have to tell me,' he said. 'Of course we're better off. Every way, we're better off. Try telling *her* that, though.'

Embarrassed for him, I got up and fetched the cups and

saucers, sugar and milk, spoons, biscuits, plates. There'd been something of angry desperation in his voice. Ever since I bought this house – more than ten years ago – the annexe has been set aside for their use. Each Easter and Christmas, a fortnight every summer, they've spent their holidays in it. It has always been understood between us that the annexe was for them to live in permanently when they became old and in need of looking after. There are no stairs to climb; it's compact and snug, completely self-contained. The old man had been delighted to come – he would have come down as soon as he retired, if he'd had his way – but from the moment they arrived with their furniture and packing-cases, my mother-in-law had been withdrawn and grim.

'I expect she's still missing her friends,' I heard Jane say. 'She'll be all right as soon as she's made some new ones.'

'Friends? What friends? She hadn't got any friends up there. All her friends had long since gone. They'd died or been rehoused in those highrise flats the other side of the borough. They'd gone away to live with their children, else, or in one of those old folks' homes, the back of beyond. *I* had friends – one or two. There was old Archie in the corner shop, and Smithy, that I worked with years ago. But I was stuck in the house all day long, wasn't I? I never got to see my two or three friends. She wouldn't let me out in case I had a fall. Four walls was all I ever saw. Your mother went out of the house, did a bit of shopping, but she had nobody to talk to except the girl at the checkout.'

'The neighbours, then.'

'You're joking! Wouldn't so much as go out in the yard if she saw any of the neighbours in theirs. Fell out with the whole bunch of them, one time and another.'

I made the tea and carried it to the table.

'It's bound to be difficult,' I said, 'learning to adjust to a new place. All the upheaval of moving.'

'I've lost count of the number of times we've moved since we were married. And that's not including being bombed out during the Blitz. God knows, she ought to be used to packing and unpacking. It's something else.'

'Prices are higher round here,' Jane said. 'No big supermarkets. Pennies on this, pennies on that. It must be a worry.' She poured the tea.

'Not that, either. Our pensions are more than enough for our needs. I can't remember when we were better off. We don't have to be all that careful with money.'

With the palms of his hands he lifted his cup. 'It's something else,' he said. 'Something else. I know what it is, too, but she'd dig up anything to moan about rather than admit it. Nothing's right for her. Doesn't like cooking with electricity instead of gas, doesn't like a shower instead of a bath. Says the bus fares are expensive. "Up in London," she says, "you can travel free if you're an old-age pensioner. You can sit on a bus all day long and not part with a penny piece. You can go right into the city, up the West End, go and look at Buckingham Palace." And she's dead right, of course, no denying it. But what she'll not tell you is that she's not gone a hundred yards on a bus these last five years to my certain knowledge. That's not what's bothering her, either.'

I drank my tea as quickly as I could. Jane and her father would have to sort out the problem between them, whatever it was. I got up and made for the door.

'It seems so ungrateful,' he said to me. 'I'm thankful to be here, though. You know that, don't you? You shouldn't have had to sweep those leaves from our path yesterday.

Difficult job for me to do, the way I'm fixed, but she could have done that.'

'It was no bother. I'd just been sweeping *our* path.'

'But it's all part of the same thing. She's not unpacked our pictures yet. I'd do it, but I'd be afraid of dropping them and smashing the glass. She's not got around to fixing the curtains properly. I wouldn't know how to do a job like sewing curtains. They look stupid, hanging down much too far. Five weeks, we've been here. Five weeks and a day. Still those curtains with frayed edges.'

'It'll all work out,' I said. 'Now I must go and finish that planting.'

Five minutes later, when I'd trodden the ground firm, I took the tools back to the shed. I'd spend twenty minutes more, I thought, before going back to the kitchen – time enough for them to talk things over. I had some tidying-up to do, and the lawn mower needed greasing over if it wasn't to rust through winter. Jane would pour a second cup for them both and then get on with her baking. A gentle rain began to fall, which would save me the bother of watering in the Peace Rose.

It was I who bought that rosebush originally. So very many years ago, that was, sometime in the sixties. Three shillings and sixpence, I paid for it. I remember counting out the coppers and small silver into the nurseryman's hand, knowing that it was about to rain and that I hadn't the fourpence left for the bus fare home. It was a spindly-looking plant, I recall: two weak stems and a rootstock like a ball of fluff. Had I known then what I know about roses now, I wouldn't have dreamed of paying good money for it. It was wrapped in a *Daily Express,* and when I stuffed it into my mackintosh pocket I pricked my thumb on a thorn. What possessed me to buy a rosebush, that autumn afternoon on my way home from work, I simply can't remember. At 24, I had no interest in gardening. The plot of ground in front of the house I'd rented was still full of decaying rubbish abandoned by the previous tenants. I had no tools – not even a spade – with which to tidy what remained of the sour and long-neglected flower beds I would be obliged, under the terms of my lease, to keep in good order. Maybe the purchase was simply a romantic and rhetorical gesture on my part. I might have been attracted by the name. *Peace, 3/6*, I'd read from the chalk scrawl at the nursery gate. Those were uneasy times. During the years I lived in that house, I was to see, successive Easters, the vastly long processions of the CND marchers passing our front window with their banners aloft; some of them – usually young mothers with children in push-chairs – would accept a cup of tea and drink it with scarcely a word, resting against our wall. It was always the Easter Sunday when they reached us, having been on the road from Aldermaston since Good Friday. On the Monday they completed the few miles into central London for the mass rally in Trafalgar Square. And there was to be a day, after I bought the rose, when I kissed my wife and children goodbye in the morning and went to work as usual, trying not to show the anxiety I felt about the American warships which would be closing upon Soviet vessels off Cuba about the time I'd be breaking for coffee. Yes – I may have bought the rose for its name. Peace was something worth paying the price of a couple of beers for. Ageing, I find it difficult to reassemble the feelings of the young man I was, but I think it quite likely that I intended the straggly bush to grow in my derelict garden as a kind of charm or talisman. Some years before, soon after our marriage, I'd sworn that I'd go to prison rather than fight Anthony Eden's war with Nasser over Suez. Now, so soon after, I was the father of three babies, poor, sharing a damp and decrepit house with my in-laws, with few prospects of ever getting out. My wife looked worn out, the children suffered from the smoggy climate of the Thames valley; it could be that the rose had more to do with my inner turmoil and despair than the world's. When I got home, I left it in its newspaper in the porch. I felt ridiculous and embarrassed about it, I suppose, because I didn't mention it to anyone, or do anything about getting it into the ground. It stayed where it was, next to the milk-bottle crate, for the rest of that week and all the next.

My father-in-law planted it. While I was out with the children on the Saturday, he borrowed a trowel from a neighbour and cleared away enough rubbish to make room for it. When I got home, I noticed it at once as I pushed the three babies in their pram up the path to the front door. No comment was passed by any of us. It wasn't until the bush bloomed the following summer that it caught my attention again. Two yellow, pink-edged flowers opened, so heavy they bowed their stems almost to the ground. The plant sent up new stems from the base, and the next summer there were to be getting on for a dozen blooms. By then my father-in-law had made the whole plot sweet and trim. Slowly we had begun to be on good terms. I learned from him how to dig, rake the soil to a fine tilth, how to sow seeds and how to thin them, how to transplant. He showed me how to prune a rosebush, cutting to an outward-facing bud with a clean, sharp knife. 'As soon as you can, you want to get away and start again,' he said. 'Save up the deposit for a house. A

couple of hundred pounds should be enough. Young people
shouldn't live with their parents or in-laws. I ought to know
– it's what I did, and it's a miserable business. I know you
were glad to have us move in with you when you took on
this house – help with the rent money and Jane's mother to
lend a hand with the kids – but you'd be better off on your
own. I'll take the lease off your hands. It'll be no trouble
finding tenants for your part of the place, if needs be.'

Another two years would elapse before we could move to
the coast. I saved what I could, month by month, but the
money accrued very slowly. I kept up the Saturday ritual of
taking the children for long outings in their pram. It gave
Jane a rest from them, and I used to love going to the river,
or to the great parks and estates that were just within walking
distance. Often we'd go to Kew Gardens, having crossed the
bridge at Richmond and followed the Thames down past
Old Deer Park and the Isleworth Eyot. Sometimes we went
as far as Richmond Park, looking out for the wandering herds
of deer, seeing the dome of St Paul's in the hazy distance
when we reached the bandstand. More often than not,
though, we went to the grounds of Osterley House. To get
there, we had to cross a busy road – the Great West Road
– which connected Heathrow airport with central London.
There would be crowds gathering along the road, sometimes,
to catch a glimpse of some celebrity who had just flown in.
Crossing that road on the way to and from work each day,
I often saw famous people being driven past. Eisenhower, I
saw, and Yuri Gagarin in his officer's uniform, standing up
in his open car to wave to us. Osterley Park, though it was
surrounded by trunk roads, factories, housing estates, was
like an idyllic, pastoral landscape out of classical literature.
There was a formal pond, full of carp and golden rudd, its

surface almost entirely covered by waterlily pads and exotic waterfowl. There were vistas of greensward, avenues of mature trees, dark thickets of rhododendron, a field or two of cows. The warden, a former policeman called Sergeant Guthrie, showed us birds' nests full of eggs: a mallard's and a barn owl's only feet apart in a hollow oak, a goldcrest's, exquisite and delicately woven into the hanging fronds of a cedar. I learned much of my natural history during those walks. 'One of these days,' I used to tell the children, 'we'll live in a place where you can see birds and fish all the time. You'll not have to walk far to see them. You'll just look out of your window, and there they'll all be.' But the truth was, I didn't believe we ever would. I used to push them home before it got dark, before the fogs began to assemble in the streets. By the time we reached the front gate, they would be fast asleep, crammed together like dolls in the pram that was getting too small for them. It wasn't until our doctor told me, of our eldest, the boy, 'This child has bronchial pneumonia, you must remove him from this house, this area, if you want him to survive,' that I began to believe there had to be a life for us elsewhere. I got myself a job in a nondescript seaside town, raked together what little money I had, borrowed fifty pounds off my father. In July, we packed our possessions into a small, rented van, drove out of the Thames valley, across the North and South Downs, and moved into a small, raw, brand-new box of a house which still smelt of new plaster and fresh paint. There, for about three years, we lived frugally until, like an unexpectedly early spring, prosperity arrived to amaze us. We bought this house, cash down, guessing the annexe would always be useful for visitors, then for our parents when they grew old.

* * *

When I went back into the house, I found Jane on her own. She was sitting at the kitchen table, reading the *Sunday Times*. I couldn't be sure, but I guessed she'd been crying.

'Your dad's gone back next door, then?' I said.

'Yes. He got upset. Didn't want you to see him in a state.'

'I've got his rosebush well and truly into the ground. That'll please him.'

'Yes.'

'I've been thinking about old times, how he planted that bush after I'd brought it home and dumped it in the porch. Remember?'

'I remember.'

'That's probably why he wanted to bring it down here. Still thinks of it as being mine, even though he's looked after it for God knows how long. I like your old man. He's one of the best.'

Jane folded the newspaper carefully into its creases, smoothing the wrinkled front page.

'We'll have to think of a way to jolly your mother along,' I said. 'We'll take them out somewhere, get them to join the Darby and Joan Club or something. She likes a game of cards. You could take her to a whist drive. She'll soon forget that slum of a place they've come from.'

'It's where they lived.'

'That's a strange thing to say. It was in ruins, nearly. Ought to have been condemned and pulled down. You heard what your dad said. There was simply nothing left for them up there.'

'But it's where they *lived*. They lived in that house much longer than they'd lived anywhere else. You know how superstitious my mother can be.'

I knew well enough. She observes all the conventional

superstitions and is forever surprising me with irrational notions I've never heard of. On the day they arrived here, when I helped to arrange their furniture in the rooms, she wouldn't hear of the beds being placed across the line of the floorboards. The bedroom is a long, narrow room; the divans would have been much more conveniently situated, had she allowed them to stay where I'd put them. 'It's bad luck like that,' was all she'd say. 'Bad luck to cross the lines.'

'I'll tell you why she won't get up of a morning,' Jane said. 'And I'll tell you why she's not bothering to unpack the pictures and alter the curtains. She's convinced that they're going to die, now they've moved here. It's not *worth* doing anything that's lasting. She's got it into her head that they should have stayed where they were. Where they *lived*. As though by coming here they're giving in. Dad's just been telling me.'

'Oh, Christ.'

'Her first words when they came. "This is where we're going to die." What can any of us do to talk her out of that?'

'I don't know. I really don't know. The trouble is, she's right. But not yet, for God's sake. Not for a long while, yet. Your dad's not as sprightly as he used to be, but she's in perfect health.'

'That's exactly what he said.'

'Don't let it upset you, love. It would have been worse, if we'd let them stay up there – another of those damp winters.'

'I asked him if that's why he brought his rosebush with him. To show her that he was thinking of the future. Something to look forward to, I mean.'

'And what did he say?'

'He said it was nothing of the sort. It hadn't crossed his

mind. And I don't believe he thinks of it as your rose still. He brought it because he's fond of it. No other reason. He said that since it's so old, it might not survive being uprooted, but it was worth giving it a try. You know my dad – there's nothing soft about him. If the damn thing dies of the frost, as it well might, he's not going to read any stupid symbolism into it. He doesn't think like that. Never has done.' She started to gather up the cups and saucers. 'All the same,' she said, 'I hope you've made a good job of planting it as you can. He said to say thanks for taking the trouble.'

We left it at that. After dinner, Jane went round to spend an hour with them. I expect she found the right words to say: common-sensical things about what her plans were for the next few days, when she'd be driving into town, how she's thinking of preparations for Christmas. She won't have said anything about death or getting old, and she won't have done any false jollying. Jane's very like her father. When she'd been gone about half an hour, I went out into the garden for a breath of fresh air. A touch of frost was crisping the grass, and the sky was clear. For a few minutes I watched them from the far side of the lawn. Light was blazing from the living-room window. I saw Jane get up and walk towards the window, stand on a chair, undo the curtain-hooks, slowly. By this time tomorrow, I guess, she'll have fixed those frayed hems.

THE INTERPRETER

Sussex contains a good many of those expensive, private boarding schools housed in converted, Victorian-Gothic mansions. The buildings, usually at the end of a long, curving, gravel drive flanked with laurel and rhododendron thickets, are seldom glimpsed from the remote lanes where their drives begin. Sometimes, though, if you drive on a bright day over the South Downs, you will see them in the valley below you.

They seem to stand aloof from the neighbouring villages. Little is known about them in their locality. Occasionally, there is a report in the local paper of some annual event in the school, but, except for the parson, who visits the school once a week to instruct the confirmation classes, and the few friends who come to take tea with the principal on summer evenings, nobody in the district has enough interest to read on past the opening paragraph. This is because, almost without exception, the pupils come from distant parts of the country, or from abroad.

A mile from the village where I live, there's a school such as I've described. It's a girls' school, named Swanley's. There are fallow deer roaming wild in the beech woods of the grounds. Sometimes I used to let my children climb over the low iron railings at the lane side so that they could follow the tracks on the deep, spongy leaf-mould to the top of the hill. Up there, just inside the edge of the wood, there is a white stone temple from which we could look out over meadow land toward the school. It always felt damp and cold in the temple, even on a hot June day; but the children liked to hide behind the pillars while they waited for me to climb the rest of the way up. The first time they did so, I found a set of antlers for them in the bracken. We never saw any deer, only their tracks, and we never saw anybody moving about in the grounds. It was as though the staff and pupils were as fugitive as the animals.

The Sunday before Christmas one year, we went through the snow up to the temple in the late afternoon when it was almost dark. My daughter Sonia, who would have been about nine, had taken to painting pictures of the school; she was entranced by the lights from two upper windows making their widening stripes of yellow over the forecourt. But her younger brothers, Michael and Jimmy, were cold and bored until they saw a car's headlights suddenly switched on outside the house several hundred yards away. We watched them flicker between black masses of heavy shrubs along the drive below us, huge, mobile glow-worms, and then we came back down the hill, and followed the fresh tyre marks to the village. We were astonished to find that, outside our house, the marks left the road and mounted the grass border by the front door; then, in a wide sweep, they regained the road and led away toward the church. Excitedly, the children crowded into the house and began talking all at once to their mother.

'Quiet!' I shouted. 'Hello, love, we've had a splendid walk in the snow. Tell me, who's just been here from Swanley's school?'

Christine smiled, incredulous. I let the children explain

to her, in short, disjointed, laughing shouts, how we knew about a visitor.

'I wasn't able to see who it was,' Christine said, 'but this had been pushed through the letter-box.' She handed me a folded sheet of paper. It said, simply, 'Please will you telephone me this evening at 6.30. F. R. Smythe (Mrs), Bursar, Swanley's School. Tel: 3027.'

'You children have got me into trouble,' I said. 'I bet somebody's seen us trespassing in the woods up by the temple. How many times have I told you not to shout and scream when we go up there?'

I rang the number while the children were having their supper.

'3027, Swanley's School. Hello?'

'Is that Mrs Smythe?'

'Speaking.'

'My name's Ashton. Earlier today I had your –'

'My note. Ah, yes. How *very* kind of you to ring so punctually.' She spoke so loudly that I had to hold the receiver well away from my ear. She sounded bossy but not unfriendly. I imagined her as big, with short-cropped hair and wearing brown tweeds.

'How can I help you, Mrs Smythe?'

'The vicar tells me that you speak some Spanish. Is that correct, Mr Ashton?'

'Well, I did once, years ago. But I've forgotten most of the little I knew. I'm afraid I wouldn't be competent to coach anybody above beginner's standard.'

So that was it: one of their pupils needed tutoring in Spanish.

She laughed very loudly, a prolonged and rasping laughter. 'No, no, no, no, *no*, Mr Ashton! Nothing like that. I just want someone to talk to the servants for me. We've got two married couples from the Canary Isles. There's only one person here who can make himself understood to them. That's Chef, and he's gone to his in-laws for Christmas. Like a fool, I forgot to ask him before he left to tell our four sunny friends that they're going to have to be here on their own for three days – Christmas Eve, Christmas Day and Boxing Day. They don't speak any English at *all*. I'm at my wit's end, Mr Ashton. There are things they must be told, things they must be asked. Do you think you could *possibly* help me out? I can't just clear off and leave them here without a word of explanation, the poor dears.'

'I'm not at all sure that I –'

'Naturally, the school will offer you a fee for your trouble. Would a token fee be acceptable to you?'

'I wouldn't dream of taking a fee, Mrs Smythe. I'd be only too willing to do what I can, but I'd have to keep looking up words in a dictionary.'

'My *dear* Mr Ashton, pray *bring* your dictionary . . .'

'Very well, I'll see what I can do, Mrs Smythe. When would you like me to come up?'

'Would this evening be quite out of the question? There's so much to be done before Christmas. I'd need to know, you see, what they'd like to have in the way of Christmas fare. Have you *any* idea what people eat in the Canary Isles at Christmas, Mr Ashton? I simply can't believe that our turkey and mince pies would be part of their culture.'

'I just can't imagine, Mrs Smythe. But they're very likely poor, and if they're poor, at home they'd probably be glad to eat whatever they managed to get hold of, Christmas or any other time. I don't see any reason why I shouldn't come up this evening. Shall we say eight-thirty?'

*   *   *

I drove up to the house amid little snowflakes which rushed into my headlights like summer moths frantic for candle flame. In places along the drive, the old laurel bushes had become straggly with neglect, and I heard their fleshy leaves paw against the side of the car. When I reached the front of the house, I saw other signs of encroaching shabbiness. Plaster had blistered away from the portico; the massive brass bell-pull hung ridiculously from a foot of feeble, rusted wire; and winter weeds protruded among long-unpruned rose bushes.

I picked up my dictionary and slammed the car door very loudly, hoping to attract Mrs Smythe's attention; I didn't want to test the frail-looking bell-pull. In the light that filtered through the stained-glass diamonds of the front door, I flicked over a few pages of the dictionary while I waited for Mrs Smythe to open the door. I heard footsteps approaching in the hall and had to be content to read only the first entry on the page I had reached: '*embarbascar*, v.t., to catch one's ploughshare in a root; to throw hellebore into the river to make the fish bite.' I was trying very hard not to laugh when Mrs Smythe turned the handle.

'Do come in, Mr Ashton. I thought I heard you arrive. What *ghastly* weather.'

I stamped the snow off my shoes and stepped inside. She was very much as I had imagined. She was indeed big and she wore a tweed suit, but her hair was fairly long and dyed that peculiar tint of blue that reminds one of charred mica. She shook my hand with a robust, wholly masculine grip.

'Oh dear, Mrs Smythe, do excuse my glove.' She hadn't given me time to pull it off. Time and again I'm forced, in this sort of way, to commit solecisms of etiquette by women who display Mrs Smythe's type of aggressive superiority.

She took no notice of my apology, but strode off down the hall. 'It's this way, Mr Ashton,' she half-shouted. Feeling surly, submissive – cowed, even – I followed her along a dim corridor that smelled like every school I've ever been in.

'I've never known the school to be so empty,' she said. 'Nearly always we have a few of the Arab girls staying at the school over Christmas, but they all seem to have found a home to go to this year. Now then, here's the kitchen. Sit you down while I try to get our Latin friends to rally round.'

I sat down at a well-scoured deal table. There were two doors set in a wall at the far end of the kitchen. Mrs Smythe rapped peremptorily on them both. 'Hello. Is there anybody there? Is there anybody *there*, I say? Hello?' She knocked on both doors again, four sharp blows executed with flawless symmetry. She turned and said, 'You don't suppose they could have gone out?' But her question was addressed to a row of copper saucepans, not to me.

I felt embarrassed by her petulance and was on the point of suggesting that I should come back the next day, when she raised her hand. 'Aha! Signs of life, I hear. At last.' She came to the table and sat down beside me. We both looked towards the left-hand door; light was now shining under it. Mrs Smythe prodded at a brittle, blue curl, one of half a dozen that stood up incongruously, like slack springs, from her otherwise straight hair. 'What an unconscionably early hour to go to bed, Mr Ashton,' she said. I smiled an answer, thinly. Light appeared under the other door. I looked at her stubby knuckles as they prinked busily from curl to curl, like science-fiction insects visiting grotesque flowers. There was a look of apologetic distaste about her as she did this;

it was as though she had imagined the two dishevelled women in those two rooms, just out of bed; and was making herself more presentable in the hope that they were doing the same. 'I ought to tell you their names before they emerge,' she said. 'The couple on the left are called Salvador – Pablo and Conchita. The other two are the Navarros. She's got an impossibly long string of names, but Chef calls her Teresa. *He*, if you please, calls himself *Jesus*. I ask you.'

I put on my glasses and fussed with the dictionary. I was very surprised when the door on the right opened and light flooded out. Mrs Smythe stood up and beckoned towards the two figures who were moving slowly towards us. Mr Navarro walked barefoot over the tile floor, just in front of his wife. He was wearing dirty corduroy trousers and a string vest. He was a young man, but his evident tiredness and expression of tight anxiety made him look haggardly middle-aged until he was close enough for me to see his good teeth, his clear brown eyes, his black hair untouched with grey. I nodded, and he nodded back.

Mrs Smythe made three abrupt stabbing movements toward the wooden bench at the other end of the table, and the couple sat down. Mrs Navarro, I now saw, was a plump girl who had probably been quite attractive a few years before. Strands of very long black hair slithered from her shoulders and partially hid the squalid nylon dressing gown she was wearing. She looked at her husband nervously, whispered something to him, and the two of them looked over their shoulders toward the other pair who had just come out of their room.

'Well, at least *they've* taken some trouble to smarten themselves up,' Mrs Smythe hissed. 'I'm sure I don't know what impression you're going to take away with you from Swanley's, Mr Ashton.' I stood up as they approached. I was stunned by the beauty of Mrs Salvador and by her husband's handsome elegance. I could tell from their slightly flushed, relaxed smiles that they had been making love. They were both dressed neatly in smart clothes; he in a light-blue suit and she in a black silk blouse and a skirt of carmine taffeta. I cleared my throat, smiled at them nervously and sat down when they did. 'Tell them who you are and why you're here,' said Mrs Smythe.

I paused for a few seconds while I fumbled for the words, and then said, 'Er, *me llamo Señor Ashton. Estoy aquí para interpretar lo que Senora Smythe va a decirles.*' Already I felt flustered. My pronunciation sounded fairly satisfactory, but the intonation was all wrong, and I felt sure that I hadn't made myself understood. I looked at their childlike faces to see how they would react. They stared back, expressionless. '*Entienden?*' I said. '*Estoy aquí para interpretar. Para traducir –*'

All four of them burst into excited chatter, cataracts of words and the frothy laughter of relief. I turned to Mrs Smythe and said, 'Heaven only knows what they're saying, but I seem to have set their minds at rest. I'm going to find it hard to understand their accent, I can tell you that.'

'Tell them that they'll be here on their own for those three days, will you, Mr Ashton?' I tried desperately to think of the Spanish for Christmas Eve. I couldn't recall it, but I thought of a way round the problem. Looking toward Mr Navarro, whose laughter had rejuvenated his stubbled face, I said: '*El veinte y cuatro, el veinte y cinco, y el veinte y seis de diciembre, ustedes . . .*' But I couldn't complete the sentence. Instead, I pointed to them one by one and said, '*Solos. Aquí.*'

When Mr Navarro put his head forward and smiled, obviously expecting a few more words to complete the sense, I pointed to them all again and, making a sweeping gesture all round me, added: '*En el colegio. Ustedes. Solos.*'

It was Mrs Salvador who came to my rescue. She nodded vigorously and then explained to the other three. Her voice disappointed me; I hadn't expected this lovely girl to have a rough, peasant slur. When she finished, she led their collective mime of comprehension.

I managed to make them understand then that they had to lock up every night. '*Con llave*,' I said, jingling my car keys in front of them. Mrs Smythe pushed a large key ring toward Mr Navarro and then held up two keys she had taken from her handbag.

'This is the key for the kitchen door,' she said. I took it from her and passed it to him; it seemed a part of my function to do so. '*Cocina*,' I said.

'And this is for the front door.'

'*La puerta principal*,' I said. Mr Navarro took the key and contemplated it with a sort of reverence. It was clearly an honour for him to be entrusted with it. He stood up and ran to his room with the keys and the ring, his bare feet slapping over the cold floor. When he came back, he was carrying a parcel tied loosely with black string. He placed it on the table and sat down.

'Whatever has the wretched man got there, I wonder?' Mrs Smythe snapped out. 'I suppose you'd better ask him in a minute. But let's settle the important business first. I'd like to know from them now what they want to eat. The headmistress left instructions that they are to have whatever special Christmas fare is appropriate to their neck of the woods – courtesy of one of our generous Middle East parents,

I may say, though there's no need for them to be told that. You could feed a regiment with that kind of money. I'll make a list, Mr Ashton.'

I now began to hate Mrs Smythe, her haughtiness, her brusque manner, her attempt to suborn me. On the other hand, I was beginning to feel the warmest affection and sympathy for the broad-smiling couples. All they asked for was a short list of simple things: oranges, a chicken, rice. Mrs Smythe sniffed her disapprobation. I pressed them to add to the list, but they seemed bewildered and too shy to ask for more.

It was then that I decided to break the cardinal rule of interpreters. Instead of remaining neutral and impersonal, I took sides. When the four of them were chatting among themselves about the parcel, I pretended that they were still talking about food.

'"Almonds," they say,' I began. And then I began to claw back from the recesses of memory the ingredients required for a *paella*: they'd like that, I thought. I'd cooked *paella* myself on several occasions. I fancy myself as a cook.

'That rice,' I said, should be the short-grained variety. And garlic – '

'I might have known,' said Mrs Smythe.

'And some diced pork, and olive oil.'

'How *ghastly*,' she said.

'And lemons, large prawns, scampi, squid – '

'*Squid?*'

'Squid. And red peppers, onions, tomatoes.'

'There are plenty of tinned tomatoes in the store.'

'Fresh tomatoes. And mussels. They have them at Tesco, Mrs Smythe. Also clams. Tesco have them, too.'

'More slowly, Mr Ashton, if you please. I can't keep up.'

I was glad to oblige her, desperate not to forget any detail. Then I remembered French beans. And saffron. Of course. *Azafrán*.

Mrs Smythe was looking appalled. When she had finished writing down the last items, she slammed down her pen.

'They must surely realise that these foodstuffs are terribly expensive, Mr Ashton? Surely a gang of illiterate peasants wouldn't indulge themselves in such luxuries, even at Christmas?'

I stared at her coldly, impertinently. 'I can assure you, Mrs Smythe, that in their own country the foods they've asked for are cheap, everyday commodities. You can hardly disappoint them now. I told them what you said – that they could have whatever they asked for. From what you told me, sufficient provision has been made.'

'I had earmarked any surplus for – but that's not the point, Mr Ashton. Food like this is wasted upon such people, despite what you say. Like feeding a donkey strawberries. You'd better ask about that sordid parcel before they ask for caviare and champagne.' Damn, I thought, I'd forgotten to ask for wine. They had to have wine, both red and white. But I judged I couldn't strain Mrs Smythe's patience any further. I'd get some wine to them, somehow.

Mr Navarro untied the string and removed the brown paper. It was a cheap pair of trainers. They were a present, he said, from the four of them to a young man who had come over on the plane with them. He was at a similar school in Surrey; Mr Navarro gave me a luggage label on which was written the young man's name and address. I imagined the five of them sharing their anxieties during the flight, and while they descended through the murky light of the Thames valley to Heathrow. The label was marked with the London address of an employment agency that specialises in foreign servants. I promised to address the parcel and post it. Thanking me profusely, Mr Navarro said that none of them could read or write; and he said how glad they were to speak to an Englishman in their own language. The chef was Portuguese, he said; they had to muddle through as best they could. My Spanish came back with a rush. Vocabulary, phrases, slang, idioms, all crowded back into my mind after years of disuse. For several minutes, while Mrs Smythe tapped her pen on the table, the talk got louder and louder, more and more animated. We talked about her; and when I mentioned the colour of her hair, and her absurd little charred-mica curls, we became downright raucous.

'What are they saying now, Mr Ashton?' she said.

'They're talking about the unbelievably strange things they've seen on their travels,' I said, 'and about how cold they find it sometimes in England.'

She stood up and pushed back her chair. She waited while I shook hands with each one of them, but she started to move away while I watched the couples going back to their rooms. They turned to wave when they reached their doors. I waved back. '*Felices Pascuas,*' I called out, as I glimpsed a crib and a little crucifix on the Salvadors' dressing-table. But they hadn't heard, and the door was closed.

I followed Mrs Smythe through the corridors to the front door. She handed me an envelope which contained, as I supposed, the fee she had mentioned. I had intended to refuse it, but I decided it could go towards the wine.

'There is just one favour I'd like to ask, Mrs Smythe,' I said as I stepped outside. 'Would it be all right, do you think, for me to walk with my children through the school grounds from time to time? We'd not come near to the house, but stay up on the hill in the woods near the old temple. I'd like my children to see the deer.'

She looked at me with contempt. 'I'm afraid that wouldn't be possible,' she said. 'We could in no circumstances countenance such a thing. We are quite strict about having outsiders within the school boundaries. We owe it to the parents, you know, to keep ourselves to ourselves. Good night, Mr Ashton, and thank you.' She shut the door.

The next morning, I went out to the car to collect the parcel and the dictionary which I'd left on the front seat. I looked in the glove compartment for the packet of Christmas cards I'd bought a few days before. Most of the cards were of snow scenes, robins, stagecoaches; but I came across one with a reproduction of Bellini's 'Madonna of the Pomegranate.' I wrote on one side:

with love and best wishes for Christmas and the New Year from your friends Pablo and Conchita Salvador and Jesús and Teresa Navarro.

On the other side, I wrote out a translation of this in Spanish. One way or another, Mr Pérez would understand; even if he, too, were illiterate, he would recognise the names Salvador and Navarro if the English version were read aloud to him.

I put the dictionary aside and wrapped the parcel securely, putting the Christmas card inside one of the shoes. As I was tying the last knot, I began to wonder about Mrs Smythe. Would she obtain those items or not? I simply could not envisage the likes of her trundling a trolley round a supermarket and asking for *squid*.

I scribbled a note to her, saying how I would write to the headmistress when the new term began, expressing the hope that her Spanish staff had enjoyed their Christmas *paella*. I would offer my services to the school, *gratis*, at any time they might be required. That should fix Mrs Smythe, I thought.

I felt my rage boiling up, on account of her forbidding me, from pure spite, to walk with my children up in those woods. She should have referred my request to the headmistress: Mrs Smythe was only the bursar, after all; a kind of go-between linking the headmistress and the outside world of tradesmen and casual callers like myself. As an intermediary, a kind of interpreter (as it seemed to me) she had grossly abused her position.

WEDDING OF STRANGERS

When I arrived with camera and guidebook at the west front of Llandaff Cathedral (this was back in the Seventies) I saw that a crowd of Saturday morning housewives was gathering. Encumbered with children, shopping-baskets and prams, they jostled good-naturedly in a tight knot of excited anticipation, waiting for the bridal party to arrive. The bells were pealing, the organ was pounding Bach through the open double doors; but it was the high-pitched gabble and chatter of the women – half in English, half in Welsh – that most impinged upon the overcast day. They craned their necks, stood on tip-toe, hopped about, stiff-legged and loud, like curious wading-birds. They seemed transfigured, eyes ablaze with the mild hysteria that possessed them, their faces vibrant and rosy, their clothes strangely vivid. Some were slapping their fretful and tugging toddlers.

The heavy August sky released its promised downpour. I raced to the shelter of a broad-leafed tree; but the women stood their ground, defying the weather. In a giggling flurry they dropped their loaded bags on to the flagstones, struggled with plastic hats and raincoats and umbrellas that blew about unmanageably. And then, reassuring each other that the shower would soon pass, they huddled together once more.

Two ushers – gawky and embarrassed in morning-dress – tried ineffectually to clear a path between them at the kerb-side. No amount of courteous wheedling would budge them from their vantage points. Smiling, but resolute, they suffered the arriving guests to barge a way through their ranks. Frantic hands clutched above the scrum at toppers and the limp, flapping brims of cartwheel hats lashed by wind and rain. A photographer, in despair, shifted his tripod several yards away.

The only other man present was the tiny old fellow who now shuffled with unhurried dignity towards me. He had neither hat nor coat. He wore a Thirties-style brown tweed suit with wide trouser bottoms and padded shoulders. Pinned to his left breast were the campaign medals of both World Wars. His sparse white hair and dark skin – puckered and velvety, like the rubbed calf binding of an ancient book – reminded me of photographs of my grandfather. Erect, arms folded stiffly in front of him, he gave me a nod as the bridegroom arrived in a Daimler with his best man. The gesture was conspiratorial, as I guessed.

'Another lamb to the sacrifice,' he said.

'Not too late, even now,' I said. 'He could run for a bus.'

'No chance, mun. Those women would tear him limb from limb. See that glint in their eyes? Like vultures at a carcass.' His voice, for someone so old and small, was surprisingly gruff and strong. I fancied he'd had a few drinks; he slurred some of his words, lurched slightly when he turned to face me. 'He'd be nothing but a heap of picked bones,' he said as I steadied him. 'Look at their scrawny necks now, and those hands like talons. You and me do well to stay out of range.' We laughed, shook hands and introduced ourselves. His name was Gwyn Meredith.

He accepted a cigarette, cupping his hard, cold hands round mine as I struck the match for him.

'Well, Mr Meredith,' I said, 'this weather's doing us no good. We'd be better off in the cathedral, in the dry.'

'Spoken like a true Englishman,' he said. 'I don't mind the rain. In Wales we know what rain is. No. It's a fancy wedding – striped trousers and clawhammer jackets. Can't go in there, looking like this. Just on a visit?'

'Yes. Thought I'd have a look at the cathedral before driving home.'

'Ah – then you're nothing to do with the wedding?'

'No. I'm a stranger here. Never been in Wales before. Came to wave goodbye to an old friend who's going to the West Indies. He sailed on the night tide from Barry. Banana boat.'

'West Indies? Warm there, mun. Nobody shivers out there. You could lie outside all night with never a stitch of clothes on you. Even the moon shines warm in the West Indies.'

'You're looking chilled, Mr Meredith. Will you come and have a drink with me? A nice pint would do us both the world of good.'

He considered the proposition for a few moments. I knew of a comfortable-looking pub not far away in Llandaff. He shook his head.

'Let's have a drop of this instead,' he chuckled; and from his inside pocket he produced a flat half-bottle of whisky. He unscrewed the top and, with a formal little bow, handed the bottle to me. I took a swig, wiped my mouth, handed the bottle back to him with a similar courtesy. 'This makes us boozing partners now,' he said, 'so whatever is said between us has to be the whole truth.' He drank a good two fingers with great relish.

By now the bridesmaids had arrived, six of them, in flimsy

pink dresses and quaint hats like sporting rosettes. Bare-armed, they flinched from the driving cold and wet, gathering their skirts and adjusting strands of hair; under two enormous golfing umbrellas held by the ushers, they looked like tropical flowers. Then the bride arrived with her father. As she stepped from the Rolls-Royce, her lace train ballooning like a spinnaker, the watching women cooed and murmured, 'There's lovely,' and in awe they stood back to allow the procession to pass by toward the darkness of the west door.

'A few months gone, would you say?' Mr Meredith asked me.

'Can't say I noticed, Mr Meredith.'

'Most of them are, mind. They try to hide it in the cut of the dress, but you can tell. Not that anybody takes that much notice these days, you understand. A white dress isn't a sign of virginity any more. Time was, a girl wouldn't have wanted to risk the bad luck.'

'Bad luck?'

'Going to the altar, pretending to be what she's not. Oh, it's not that I have any *moral* objection. All I'm saying is that people forget what symbols mean. These women, now, that always come to gape at a wedding – they're such fools. They think it'll bring them luck to see a bride all in white. But it doesn't count, see, if the girl's not a virgin. So they're just wasting their time, and serve them right!' He cackled delightedly, handing me the bottle. 'Not that I'm superstitious, mind,' he added.

The congregation and choir had begun to sing 'Dear Lord and Father of Mankind.' Arms outspread, Mr Meredith beat time with graceful flourishes. The sleeves of his jacket rode up nearly to his elbows, revealing frayed and much-darned shirt cuffs. As the wind gusted or fell slack, so the music died or swelled in the cathedral close. At times the organ and the thin voices were entirely lost for a few bars while the branches thrashed above our heads. Some of the women tittered and nudged their neighbours at the sight of a tipsy and threadbare old man conducting; but Mr Meredith was impervious. With ever more sweeping gestures and elegant posturings he held the steady beat of the tune, humming the bass harmony until the final verse, which he sang in unison. His eyes, after the last sustained chord had dispersed in the wind, were glistening. 'One of the truly great hymns,' he pronounced. 'They couldn't have chosen better.' He took the bottle from me and refreshed himself.

'I could tell how much you enjoyed it.'

'I love to hear the music. Whenever there's a recital I come.'

'Do you go to the services?'

'Services? Oh dear me, no. I'm *Chapel*, you understand. A man must keep loyal. But – ah – the music, mun. They've got a lovely organ here. And a choir that would make the very angels weep with joy. There's nothing I like better than to come and listen to the music after I've had a walk in the Fields and a read of the paper. Not just today – every Saturday. There's always something going on.'

The rain was easing. Some of the women, pointing out patches of blue sky between the flying storm-clouds, took off their plastic hats and shook them. Not many had left when the ceremony began; others, returning from the shopping centre, had increased the size of the crowd. Less vociferous now, they waited for the wedding party to emerge. They shared a kind of obdurate bonhomie as the minutes went by, patient and gritty as a wartime queue outside a shop. Each one guarded her square yard of territory.

'Are you a married man?' Mr Meredith asked me. 'Not that you must think me nosy.'

'No, Mr Meredith.'

'Call me Gwyn.'

'How about you?'

'Ay,' he sighed. 'I was a boy, still in my teens. And the day after the wedding I left for the War.'

'That was hard.'

'Hundreds of us did the same. 1918 it was – but of course we weren't to know it would soon all be over. I was old enough to be called up, so off I went. But there was this girl, see? She lived high up in the valley. I scarcely knew her, except to smile at after Chapel. We were daft, mun. Daft and young and married before you could say knife. We hardly said a word to each other. I never knew what she was thinking, or what she felt – she was that shy. Wait a bit, now, and I'll show you her likeness.'

From his wallet he took a sepia photograph, much creased and faded. The image of the girl was little more than a milky blur, but I could tell how beautiful she must have been. She was in her wedding-dress, holding a spray of roses.

'I see she's all in white, Gwyn. Nice. She's lovely.'

'My mother's dress. She made Branwen have it. Insisted.'

'Well, women are sentimental about such things.' I gave back the photograph and tried to picture him as a young man in uniform. His eyes were moist once more. His face twitched as he put his wallet away.

'But she had no *business* to wear it, you see?' he said. 'Not white. But you don't want to hear all about that.'

'Come on, Gwyn. We're boozing companions now, like you said.'

'Well, my Branwen – I think she was more ashamed of

135

what folks might say if she *didn't* wear the white dress. Frightened out of her wits, she was, standing at the altar. A brave girl, though. Didn't give the game away when she ran the gauntlet of the women outside. None of them could guess.'

'And then you went straight to France?'

'Ay. And came back to Wales eight months later to find she'd just been rushed into hospital. A girl-child, it was, born with something wrong, and Branwen herself at death's door. And I'd fought in the trenches, and not a scratch on me. The third day I went, a doctor said to me, "Mr Meredith," he said, "I'm sorry to have to tell you your daughter has died." Then he asked if I minded if they used her little body for medical research. He took me into his office and I signed the form. Branwen was a bit better by now, but she didn't know who I was. I was like somebody she'd never set eyes on before. I had to tell her, see, about the baby.'

'That's awful, Gwyn. Very sad. Here, have a cigarette and we'll listen to this hymn.'

This time he didn't conduct, or sing, or even hum. It was a hymn whose melody was strange to me, and as far as I could tell it was sung in Welsh. Deep in his thoughts, Mr Meredith nodded in time with the music or tapped out the beat with his toe. The sun had begun to shine hot on the women. We remained under the dripping tree.

'A little boy,' he said. 'We had a little boy about a twelvemonth after. Branwen never got right, though. No.'

'I'm sorry.'

'My married sister brought him up. Like her own son he came to be. Oh, he always knew who I was, of course, but they lived a good way off and I never saw much of him. I was single-handed on the farm, see, once Branwen had died, and I couldn't leave the cows. My sister gave him his name – Denzil. He turned out to be a bright boy, went to college and all. He's a big man now, in Cardiff. Has his own business, employs a lot of men. All turned out well, in the end.

'Do you see much of him?'

'Not too much. Too busy, see? A business is like a farm, you can't leave it. Christmas-time, he might drop in. But he doesn't bring his family. There'd not be room, he says, in my little cottage.'

'Live on your own, then?'

'Other side of Llantrisant. Fair way.'

'Must be lonely for you.'

'No, no. There's always something to do. Things to mend, books to read, the wireless to listen to. Then there's Chapel, Sunday mornings and evenings. But Saturdays are best. Rain or shine I get the bus and come into town. When I've had my walk I come and listen to the organ and sit in the Memorial Chapel for a while. You'll see it when you go in.'

'I'll look out for it.'

'I read the names, see, of all my friends that fell. They're all there, the ones that didn't come back. The Welch Regiment, you know. All my pals. And they're still the best pals I ever had. One especially – Jackie Jones. "It'll be no good if I ever get home out of this mud," he said to me, "I'll never get warm again." And then he died of his wounds. He was a real good pal. I've always had good pals.'

'Well, Gwyn, I'm glad you were one of the lucky ones. Let me take your picture.'

He stood to attention for me, anxious that the sun should strike his medals. I wanted him to smile, but I didn't ask him to. Instead, I caught an expression of pride and defiance.

'I think about her, too, in there – Branwen, I mean,' he

said as he relaxed. 'About the two of us, married, and with children to our name, and still no more than strangers. How I'd come unharmed out of the worst war in history, and how she died of silly women's superstition. She did, you know.'

'Come on, Gwyn. You said you didn't believe all that old nonsense.'

'I don't, I don't, nor ever did,' he said with sudden vehemence. 'But I know that my Branwen did. It was all there in the letters she wrote to me in France. She was just an ignorant country girl, with her head full of her mother's claptrap and old wives' tales. All that fear and guilt's what destroyed her. If that first baby had lived, maybe she would have, too. Sort of thing couldn't happen these days, thank God.'

His eyes blazed with his conviction and he had begun to tremble. For a minute or two we stood together in silence, watching wisps of steam rise from the drying pavement. I lit a cigarette, embarrassed by the passion my lack of tact had provoked. He drank the last of the whisky, threw the empty bottle in a bin. When his rage subsided, he turned to me and smiled as though apologetically.

'Take no notice of me,' he said, 'I get too worked up sometimes.'

'So what do you do with yourself after you've been in the Memorial Chapel?' I asked him.

'Oh, it's great, mun, after! I go to the pub and have a glass or two. More times than not I get talking to somebody – like it might be you, today – and we make friends. I've got hundreds of friends. Always somebody to talk to and help pass the time. Best part of my life, since I've been retired.'

*　　*　　*

Soon, the marriage service was over. The double doors were thrown open and a jubilant anthem blared through. We watched as the photographs were taken: the customary stilted poses of bride and groom and all the possible combinations of groups from both families. Most of them looked prosperous in an unsympathetic way; hard, and hard-bitten, smiling like dolls. Then, in small blizzards of confetti, the couple left for the reception in their Rolls, quickly followed by several carloads of bridesmaids and close family guests. Dozens more streamed past us up the hill on foot. The women spectators, the mystery of their vigil now over, quickly dispersed.

The man I had identified as the bride's father while the photographs were being taken remained at the gate, talking urgently to the ushers. Now and again he looked in our direction. I imagined he had taken me for one of the guests – a friend of the groom, maybe – who had arrived late for the ceremony. Now, grey topper in hand, he came towards us. His eyes avoided mine as I prepared to speak to him. It was Mr Meredith he spoke to.

'Daddo,' he said, 'I didn't know you were out here. I thought you weren't coming at all when you didn't reply to the invitation. Look at you – you got drenched out here.' And with a grimace he held Gwyn's sleeve between thumb and forefinger.

I suppose I should have moved away. The old man looked cowed, a frail stick beside this big, florid son of his.

'I didn't like to go in,' he said feebly. 'You understand, Denzil. Not like this. Not with all your friends in their posh clothes.'

'You've been drinking, Da, haven't you?'

'I didn't think anybody would miss me, Denzil. But I've

been here all the time. I saw everybody arrive and I watched them all leave. I listened to the service, the hymns. I sent a little present.'

'Your grand-daughter would have liked to have you at the ceremony, you know. It wasn't much to ask.'

'She's got her husband. That's what counts. I've been talking to this gentleman.'

'You must excuse my father,' Denzil said to me. 'He will insist on pestering strangers. Excuse me, I must hurry on to the reception. You're welcome to come, Da, if you will.'

He turned, strode to the car the ushers were waiting in.

'You mustn't mind Denzil,' Gwyn said to me, leading the way to the cathedral door. 'It's just his way. Now then, you go and take your snaps while I sit down for a few minutes. Then we'll go and have that pint.'

PRESENT, SIR

Not far short of half a century on, I can still recite the names. Indeed, I often do. When I'm waiting, with nothing to read – for sleep, for news – I repeat them. Like an incantation, or a mantra, they keep at bay boredom, anger, panic, fear. Some people have recourse to yoga, or exotic forms of meditation, else find comfort in counting slowly to ten. And some, perhaps, take deep breaths while imagining the scent of roses. I call a roll of thirty sixteen-year-olds in alphabetical order. The names (surnames only: no given names or even initials, we never used them) are chiselled deep into a slab of my mind as unremoveable as a war memorial. Inexplicably, they are a comfort. In the register, of course, they would have appeared as one long list down the page; and, as the year progressed, against each one there would have grown a red herring-bone, perhaps interspersed with black rings. But I write them down in a double column, pairs of names, answering the insistent rhythm of the found poem they speak to the inner ear.

> Ayling, Bassnett;
> Bee, Bennell;
> Bennett, Butler;

Coleman, Crowhurst;
Dingemans, Groves;
Hall, Hayter;
Heath, Jary;
Lewin, Mercer;
Moxham, Moyle;
Pickett, Potter;
Potter, Robinson;
Sayer, Sherlock;
Turrell, Tweed;
Upperton, Walker;
Wilmshurst, Wood.

And, as I write them down, I notice just *why* the rhythm is insistent. Old skills of the *lecture expliquée* return after long neglect. Each name of more than one syllable (with the single exception of *Bennell*) has the stress fall on the first syllable. How skilful the poet has been to insinuate that one exception so near the beginning! One is seduced into expecting a similar eccentricity to occur again somewhere before the piece concludes, thus mitigating what would otherwise be a steam-rollering monotony. The seven single-syllabled names, rather less than a quarter of the total number, are introduced not in a regular or symmetrical pattern but – more subtly – where they are required as strong key-stones in what could otherwise have been a toppling masonry of trochees and dactyls. The final monosyllable *Wood* is an apt pun, if we were to take the liberty of mixing our architectural metaphor and think of it as the massive king-post of foursquare oak on which the rest of the poem's roof-span depends for its strength. And how technically satisfying is the repetition of *Potter*, forming, as it does, a kind of mortar of *enjambement* between the first two-thirds of the piece and the final third: one is reminded of the effect of the octet and sestet of the Petrarchan or Italian sonnet: the wave forming and gathering; and then, once broken, receding.

Yet Wood, the boy whose name this was, was no stout, fine-grained character. When I appraise the thirty images of this poem – really get to grips with them instead of reeling them off mindlessly, parrot-fashion – I find some of them vividly evocative, others perversely obscure or irrelevant. Wood, who has supported all that weight for so many years, was a twig of a boy. He was inconspicuous to such an extent that he escaped the attentions of bullies. And yet I remember him clearly; and now that I can give his name flesh, I want him to be a corporate executive wielding very considerable power with exquisite compassion, a Heart of Oak. And Wilmshurst, who sat next to him – who assembled radio sets out of jagged strips cut from cocoa-tins – let him be prosperous and happy and endlessly fulfilled with his inventiveness. I thank him for his soothing name; gentle, soft, a hamlet of thatched cottages in summer. I am indebted to them all, for they are part of the compacted archaeology (for I am getting old now) of my life. They are always accessible for excavation whenever I need them, names to relish not just for their textures in the mouth but also for the one or two facts I can recall about each of them but one:

Ayling was 'interfered with' by a French master with a double-barrelled name who was sacked and who subsequently played piano in the Brighton Hippodrome orchestra.

Bassnett, acneous, greasy-haired, down-at-heel, said he would never revisit the school as an old boy unless as a millionaire who could arrive in his own Rolls-Royce. I'm told that he did, aged twenty-two.

Bee was ginger and densely freckled, and had a much younger brother twice his size, dark and *un*freckled. So, up to a point, they were lucky. What every man could do with is a sister. Mine died, a three-week baby. I have begun to mourn her, now she'd have been in her fifties.

Bennell, even then, was balding; unathletic by temperament, he would yet challenge the best sprinters in the school to a race over *ten yards* and always win.

Bennett had the raw, brutish and vacuous face of a peasant. He was docile and refined, but we imagined him in a spattered smock, by moonlight, feeding human babies to pigs in a lost valley of the Vaucluse.

Butler, red and round as a harvest moon, practised steps of Olde Tyme dancing in empty classrooms at lunchtime. His Dinky One-Step was nifty, considering his bulk. He danced with a chair.

Coleman, dusky, may have been related to some people of that name, a farmer and his wife who rode to hounds, in whose house died, in 1945, Lord Alfred Douglas. Lord Alfred's last words (they told me) were, 'what won the three-thirty?'

Crowhurst was born when his father was in his seventies. Crowhurst himself looked very old and always took the old-man's part in school plays. The make-up, applied by the headmaster's wife, enhanced and emphasised his features rather than disguised them. (I saw him recently. He looked much younger than I.)

Dingemans – three syllables, the g is hard – was the son of a well-off doctor. He had come from some private school, spoke cut-glass. By the end of the year, now fluent in the Sussex dialect and coarsened in his manners, he was removed to some other, private, school. He taught me the word *lèse-majesté*.

Groves was nicknamed Needle. He had a hole in his head, he maintained. I liked Groves, and hardly ever spoke to him.

Hall, before emigrating to Australia, broke four desks and seven chairs into pieces small enough to poke through the rotting floorboards of room 9. In Australia I have breathed in the scent of eucalyptus, and found it heavenly; and, once, I was almost killed by a branch falling unannounced from a gum-tree. The smell of slow rot is not entirely unappealing.

Hayter was hated for killing and mounting in cardboard boxes rows and rows of identical butterflies. Whenever I read 'The Love Song of J. Alfred Prufrock' and come to the lines –

> *And when I am formulated, sprawling on a pin,*
> *When I am pinned and wriggling on the wall,*

– I hate Hayter with a redoubled hatred: for I have to put down the book, and muse upon the fact that Hayter looked

like the young Eliot (whose overcoat I once tried on in Faber
& Faber's offices, not long after his death.)

Heath spent break-times and lunch-times in the lavatories
with Lewin: not closeted, but indulging in roustabout horse-
play to the continuo of hissing cisterns and within the carry
of stale urine.

Jary was the only Jew in the form. I learned what anti-
semitism was from the moment that the music master
said, in front of the class, 'Oh, how I hate your sort,
Jary.' I wanted to like Jary; to atone for the cruelty he suffered, with small, sentimental gestures of kindness. But the
fact was that Jary, as it happened, was impossible to like.
On account of Jary, I describe myself as a bleeding-heart
liberal.

Lewin, bosom chum of Heath, joined the R.A.F. Within six
weeks he was killed in a Mosquito that crashed in sight of
the school.

Mercer taught me everything I know about astronomy. He
filled blackboards with patterns of stars; red giants and
romantic constellations which, to this day, I can drop casually
into dinner-party conversations. Nearly everything else I was
taught that year has been sucked into that ravenous Black
Hole where all my facts are crammed into a tiny ball, hid-
eously dense.

Moxham belonged to the Plymouth Brethren. He told us
how they sat in a tin shed on top of the South Downs for
hours and hours on Sundays. Sometimes not one of them

would utter a single word. I wouldn't mind having a tin shed up there: but with room for only one.

Moyle, clean-cut, brisk, practised bowlines and sheepshanks with a length of cord he always kept in his pocket. I know how to tie a hangman's knot. (With a Staffordshire knot, you can hang three men at a time.) The old skills, one comes to believe, should not become utterly redundant.

Pickett (nicknamed, wittily, Won't-Get-Well-If-You) became a pharmacist. His name evokes the smell of pink healing ointment.

Potter (i) came from Epsom and, the year before, had tipped the winner of the Derby. I won fourteen shillings on Nimbus, thanks to him. I've been lucky all my life; but, as Potter (i) warned me, no man's luck can last for ever. That fourteen bob, invested at compound interest, would have procured more than an adequate quietus.

Potter (ii), no relation, was my closest friend that year. The first time I got drunk was in his company. We put away nine pints of black-and-tan in a pub by the river Adur. Here, Charles II almost fell into the Roundheads' hands during his flight to France. Re-enacting the scene after closing-time (Potter played the king) I, a suspicious soldier, chased His Majesty over the bridge, tackled him, and was pulled over the parapet into the icy waters. Neither of us can be certain who saved the life of whom. Certain it is that we could have killed each other.

Robinson's ghost will not return. Not a shred of him clings to the memory. Robinson, therefore, is that most frightening of phantoms; just beyond the edge of vision, he disappears as I turn my head. (But, N.B: when, lately, I happened to read this piece aloud to an audience in Folkestone, I was mortified when, after the questions-and-answers session, a gentleman approached me and announced that he was Robinson. This seemed an inventive, and witty, thing to do. But I have ascertained, since, that he was, indeed, Robinson. He *was*. And, though I still cannot reassemble him during my waking hours, I often glimpse him in my dreams; and I wake up, terrified.)

Sayer is in mid-air, his shooting foot pointed dead ahead, his left leg straddling an imaginary hurdle. The football has slithered against the goal-netting, has rotted and perished in a locker-room, has been thrown out with the sweepings of countless soccer seasons. But Sayer still hovers, still as a kestrel, performing one action perfectly: which is more than most men can expect to do during one lifetime.

Sherlock, too, is on the soccer field, playing beside me in the half-back line. It is ten years after we left the school, but my retina retains the sixteen-year-old image of him. The team we are playing for is called The South-Eastern Gas Board Reserves. We are guest players. I realise that it is time to hang up my boots.

Turrell ate, as I did, meat-extract sandwiches. When we opened our lunch-boxes, the classroom was suddenly filled with the odour of poverty.

Tweed was in every way symmetrical. Ambidextrous, he had a centre parting in his hair, and he did up *all* the buttons of his jacket. He saw both sides of any argument. His rare, pinched smile suggested incipient madness. But he is still as sane as they come, and I have evidently been wrong about the likes of him.

Upperton was asked to leave, for crimes as various as arson, petty pilfering, and playing eight-to-the-bar. Not long afterwards I met him in the High Street. He was wearing his army uniform. It included a cockade of handsome feathers, and he'd just been decorated for extreme gallantry on active service in Korea. Now he is (I hear) something of a recluse, living on a converted minesweeper, which lists on the mud at low tide. He was one of the three most brilliant people I have known in my life, and I wish I had the courage to tread across his deck and knock on his equivalent of a front door, a hatch-cover.

Which leaves *Walker*, whoever he was. I suppose that the name produces a vignette in the mind of a Tweed *(he was so-so)* or a Robinson *(he was substantial)*. All I can remember is a prevailing wind of anxiety. Adults would say, 'Make the most of these times, they're the happiest years of your life.' And I would think, if that is so, I should cut my throat this minute. I know that it was the year I lost my virginity. I know that twice I fainted in that classroom, my head cut open by the flanges of the radiator, so overcome was I by the sudden hot onrush of fear that I had made my girl pregnant. And afterwards, every day for several weeks until I heard that she was all right, I could only stave off another fainting fit by rattling off everything that came to my mind that I'd learned by heart. Rehearsing in my head how I'd break the news to my implacable mother that I'd got a girl 'in trouble' or 'in the family way' I would begin to feel trembly and incoherent. The cosine rule was a straw to grasp; then the theorem of Pythagoras, swiftly followed by *towns, small islands, domus and rus;* John of Gaunt's patriotic speech from 'Richard II' steadied me, and Ohm's Law and the masculine French nouns ending in *-ion* helped my breathing. When I received the note from the girl (it was carried by Butler, who had acquired the On Leave Foxtrot the evening before) I was seven stanzas into 'The Rime of the Ancient Mariner.' 'Everything okay,' the note said, and the spasm of relief did not subside until Mr Goble came to call the register.

Goble's voice was mannered – downright theatrical, sometimes, when he read out our names at the beginning of the afternoon session. He liked two or three pink gins with his lunch. His affectations were a delight to me; and it's his RADA tones I hear when the list runs through my memory, like the complete soundtrack of a film that has decayed in its can, except for a few frames of chaotic footage. 'Ayling, Bassnett, Bee, Bennell,' I have him say while I have a chest X-ray; 'Bennett, Butler,' as the 747 begins its descent; 'Wilmshurst, Wood,' he concludes as the plate is clear, or the safety-belt slackens, and everything, yet again, against all the odds, is okay, okay, okay.

THE ARIEL

'He's in his chair,' Mum told me at the garden gate. 'He'll
be glad to see you. Sit and talk to him for a bit while I go
and do the shopping.'

'How is he?'

'Downright miserable – says he's sick of people trying to
cheer him up. Snaps your head off at the least thing. It's
hard to know *what* to say to him, so be careful.'

'Doctor been?'

'About an hour ago.'

'What's he say?'

'Says he's doing fine but he's got to be patient.'

'Well, he knew all along it'd be a longish job. Bound to
take time, learning to walk again. He said so himself before
he went in for the operation.'

'But if you remind him he gets very bitter. Says he'd
sooner have put up with the pain than be stuck on those
crutches months on end.'

'It's just depression. After all, he's only been home a few
days. Everybody's like that. In a day or two –'

'That's what the doctor said.'

'He couldn't have been in better hands. Just about the
best hospital in the country. He'll find it's worth it to be

shot of that arthritis. It hurt me just to look at him walking about half crippled. How many years is it?'

'More than I can remember.'

'If he can be patient that long, what's another couple of months?'

'I know. See if you can talk some sense into him while I'm out. Make a pot of tea – you know where everything is. And give him one of his tablets. They're behind the clock. I must fly – here's the bus coming.'

She ran through a gap in the traffic. When she was on the bus, she waved from the back window. She looked tired; it must have been a difficult week for her.

His eyelids were shut too tight. I sat down opposite him, and waited for him to pretend to wake up; it's been a convention of ours, ever since I was a little boy and used to climb into bed between him and Mum first thing in the morning. He was wearing the blazer I'd given him. The black doeskin was in sharp contrast with his hair, which didn't look grey any more but a loose, dry white. Usually he kept it greased, shining and darker. I wondered how long it had been as white as that. His crutches, propped against the table between us, were the colour of his hair as I was used to it – aluminium grey, with silver flecks that shone when the light fell at a sharp angle. I'd have to get accustomed to his looking older. He shifted in his chair, clasped his hands under his right knee, and sat forward.

'Oh,' he said. He sucked in breath against a sudden pain, and then breathed out slowly, his lips pushed forward as if he was trying to whistle. 'So it's you, then.'

'Hello, Dad. I thought we might go for a run along the beach, as far as Splash Point. What will you give me, a five-minute start?'

'Look, for Christ's sake don't *you* try to jolly me along. I've had enough of people this week coming in and saying daft things like that.'

'All right, then. You look terrible, at death's door.'

'Ha blasted ha. Do something useful. Go and put the kettle on. And make it good and strong.'

'You'll poison yourself, one of these days.'

'Might as well, all the good I am like this.'

I went into the kitchen, filled the kettle, and plugged it in. His pint mug and my mother's flowered cup and saucer were set out on the yellow oval tray I'd given them a few Chrismases ago. I remembered the tin of tobacco I'd brought for him. That might cheer him up, though in our family we've always been shy about giving and receiving presents. We send them by post, or leave them lying about the house, rather than hand them over in person. When I gave him the blazer, I left it on the doorstep after dark, wrapped in brown paper. I didn't even put in a note. If I'd brought it round and asked him to try it on, he'd have said, 'I can't take all your clothes off your back.' And then the blazer would have hung for years in my wardrobe. Leaving it on the doorstep was the only acceptable way. I looked at him through the living-room door. There he was, wearing the blazer in my presence, and he'd just asked me to make him a cup of tea. Instead of hiding the tobacco under his pillow, as I'd intended, I'd give it to him now. I skimmed the tin along the carpet, so that it came to rest within his reach, next to his crutches.

'There you are, you miserable old devil,' I said. 'Something for you.' Before he had time to look in my direction, I went back to the kettle. It had come to the boil.

'There was no need for this!' he shouted. 'No need at all. It's a *two-ounce* tin, goddam it.'

'You can smoke yourself to death.'

I made the tea. While it was brewing, I watched him pick up the tin, open it, smell the tobacco, and then put it out of sight beside his chair, under a newspaper. I poured the tea and put four heaped teaspoons of sugar in his mug. I didn't stir it but left the spoon standing in it, almost submerged. 'Here you are, then,' I said, carrying in the tray. 'It's so thick fur could grow on it.'

'Have you stirred it up?'

'Hell, what do you take me for? Stir it yourself. And get that pipe lit. You don't look right, sitting there without it.'

'No, I won't for a bit. Not been able to enjoy a proper smoke since I came to after the operation. Nothing tastes the same. Wish to God I'd never had it done. Don't think I'll ever get right. Should have left well alone. Want the spoon?'

'I don't take sugar. You know that.'

'Dunno how you can suffer it without.' He took the spoon from his mug and laid it on the newspaper. I watched the spread of the little brown stain.

'I daresay it's the anaesthetic,' I said.

'What is?'

'In your bloodstream still, making everything taste funny.'

'Ah.'

'It hangs around for days. Probably makes you feel depressed, too. But don't give in to it. Light your pipe, try to get back to normal.'

'No good. I've tried. Tastes like old rope.'

'Then try again.'

'Can't. Left my pipe in the bedroom.'

'I'll go and get it for you.'

'You won't, then. I can manage quite well, thank you. I'll go myself.'

The crutches clanked against themselves as he heaved himself up from the chair and fitted them to his arms. He balanced on his good leg for the several seconds it took him. We would both have been appalled if I'd had to help him. 'Blasted things,' he said, swaying unsteadily, 'blasted tin legs. Who'd have thought it? *Me* on blasted tin legs.' He moved away on them, with an ease that astonished me, toward the passage.

He came back, with the pipe sticking out of the breast pocket of his blazer. He fell on to his chair, letting the crutches clatter to the floor. The sudden jarring of his hip hurt him, and he gasped.

'You've got to take one of your tablets, Mum said.'

'They're no damn good. I shan't.'

'Take it, or I'll kick your bad leg.'

'Give it here, then. Can't expect any sympathy from you.'

'What do you mean, *sympathy*? I'm your son, aren't I? What's a son for if he can't kick his father's leg when he wants to? Is it very bad?'

'Terrible.'

'I know. But you're supposed to say it's getting on fine.'

'Well it doesn't feel like it's getting on fine. By Christ it doesn't.'

'Still no reason why you shouldn't *say* it's getting on fine. Listen, remember when I was a nipper and just had my tonsils out? You kept on asking me if I'd got my voice back, and I had to keep on writing "Yes" on bits of paper.'

He smiled, looking away from me.

'Right, then. Take that tablet. You've still got some tea left. Swallow it with that.'

He did. 'I'm not sure it isn't these things that are getting me down,' he said.

'If they do, then they're probably meant to. Painkillers. Anyway, apart from the fact that you've been hacked about and stuffed to the ears with drugs, what's the news?'

'Old Charlie next door's got gout. Give us one of your rotten matches to light this thing.' I threw him the box. 'And Mrs Ogden's died.'

'Mrs Ogden?'

'The old girl with the dogs. You *know*. Funeral's tomorrow. I'll have to find somewhere else to keep the old bike.'

'The old Ariel? Surely it isn't still in Mrs Ogden's garage?'

'Course it is. Where else would it be?'

'Nowhere. But I thought you'd got rid of it years ago.'

'You thought wrong, then.'

I remembered him acquiring his first car, a Mini Traveller. 'It's *thirty years*,' I said.

'What is?'

'I've worked it out. It's thirty years – must be – since you put that museum piece in Mrs Ogden's garage. Thirty-*five*, even!'

'Ah. Daresay.'

'When was the last time you went and had a look at it?'

'Never have done. I took it there, left it, and haven't been back since.'

'But you used to love that old bike. It might have been a pet animal, the way you cared for it.'

'Well, I would have done, I suppose. But then your ma fell out with Mrs Ogden, so I didn't like to go. I hadn't thought about it much lately, to tell the truth – not until the old girl snuffed it. I expect it won't be long before the house is sold, so I'll have to think of somewhere else to keep it. Can't bring it here! Your ma used to curse that bike when it stood in the outhouse, where the carport is now. It was always in the way. I've always wanted a proper garage of my own, a little lock-up workshop. I could have enjoyed myself for hours, tinkering with the engine. You can't do a proper job in the back yard or on the kitchen table. Mind you, I had that bike going sweet as a Swiss watch right up to the day I took it to Mrs Ogden's.'

'Tell you what. Let's go and have a look at it. Got the key? You could manage that far, couldn't you?'

'I shouldn't. I'm supposed to stay sat here.'

'Scared of being hen-pecked, are we?'

'Do as I like, and don't you forget it.'

'Right, then. Mum's going to be ages yet. It's only a few yards. Bring your pipe. Still not lit it, have you?'

I waited for him in the garden while he searched through the cases under his bed for the key. God knows how he was going to manage. I'd give him five minutes. If he hadn't come outside by then, I'd just have to go and help him. But the thought alarmed me. When I was fifteen or so, he fell off a ladder while he was painting the upstairs windows. As I ran to help him, he bawled out. 'Don't get in the way, silly young devil: go and tell your mother I'm trying to get up, and tell her to put the kettle on.'

He came out, carrying the key between his teeth. There was fluff from under the bed all over his blazer. I took the key from his mouth and put it in my pocket.

'I could have carried it,' he said.

'I know. I wanted to talk to you. Hey, do you reckon the bike's still there? Suppose she gave it away for scrap?'

'We'd better get a move on and find out.'

Usually, we keep in step when we walk along together. I found myself trying to take strides as long as the reach of his crutches. He used them with an expertise that reminded me of his carpenter's skill with tools, but he spread them unnecessarily wide so that there was not quite enough room for me to walk on the path. When we reached the garage, I undid the padlock and followed him into the half-dark.

'Well, damn my rags. She's still there – look,' he said.

At first, all I could see was a heap of sacks and old coats, but then under them I glimpsed a square inch of licence plate.

'See that? VP –'

'9805,' I said. 'Let's get the trappings off, then. Bet she's smothered with rust.'

'You're on. The tyres might be a bit sad after all this time, but I gave all the metal parts a good greasing over. Stand back. I need some room.'

He propped himself on one crutch, using the other to lift the coverings. They dropped on the floor, with little explosions of dust. He went red in the face, trying not to cough. I looked round the garage for a light switch but couldn't find one. I opened the double door wide, and wedged it with a half brick. Back inside, I found him leaning against the wall near the bike. He'd found the light switch; a frail, yellowy glow was seeping from a cobwebbed bulb just above his head.

He began to fill his pipe. I took out my handkerchief and dusted the saddle. I used to sit on that saddle for hours when I was a small boy. I could just reach the handlebars if I lay along the tank in a racing position. Sitting on that scallop-shaped saddle, alone in the cluttered outhouse, I'd let my fantasies swamp over me. The machine had been battleship, castle, castaway raft, an elephant, and all the horses I had ever read about – Bucephalus, Rosinante, and the Lone Ranger's Silver. Sometimes, when the TT races were being held in the Isle of Man, or when I'd seen Dad ride past the house at full throttle along the Brighton Road, my dreaming turned it back into the powerful motorbike it was. In my goggles and shining leathers, I'd scream round tight corners in quiet villages and make brief refuelling stops in busy pits. I must have ridden that bike farther and harder than Dad. It had taken me up mountains, across deserts, under oceans, and even through the soft white dust of the moon.

I shook the handkerchief and put it back in my pocket.

'See? I told you. Not a trace of rust,' Dad said. He scraped a thin line through the grease that coated one of the exhaust pipes: chromium glinted the length of the mark he made with his crutch on the silencer. 'Not in bad shape, is she, considering she's such an old lady? Better than me. Come to think of it, this bike's got a lot to answer for. Probably started off the trouble with my leg.'

'How do you mean? Getting yourself wet, riding through the rain?'

'No, not that. Mind you, I expect that didn't do much to help. But not long after I'd bought it – sometime in 1930, I think it must have been – I fitted a high-compression piston and quick-lift cams. It was already a fast bike, but I had to try and get an extra ten miles per hour. So, ever after that, whenever I kick-started her, she kicked me back.'

'I used to pretend the bike was a mule,' I said, 'loaded up with stuff to take across a mountain pass into Tibet. What was that film called? You know, the one where the plane crashes in the snow and all the survivors are taken to a monastery?'

'Don't know.'

'Yes, you *do*. It was on television a little while back. An old, old film. One of the early talkies, shouldn't wonder. So you're bound to remember it.'

'I was nineteen when I bought it. Cash down. Forty-eight pounds ten shillings, plus five guineas for lights.'

'You're always telling me how hard up you were in those days.'

'I was. We all were. But you were nobody if you hadn't got a bike. Most of the lads bought them on the never-never, but your grandfather made me save up every penny until I could pay cash. He didn't approve of buying on the drip-feed.'

'What did you do then, you and the other lads? Terrorise small towns, like Marlon Brando?'

'Who?'

'Marlon Brando.'

'I used to go with Trunkie Jennings to the dirt-track meetings. He rode as an amateur, and I got in free as his so-called mechanic-helper. You've met old Trunkie, haven't you? Did I ever tell you how I first met him?'

'No.'

'Well, one day I'm riding along, nice and steady, and Trunkie overtakes me. And he's standing on the saddle, with his arms waving up and down, like an eagle.' Balancing on his good leg, Dad spread his crutches wide and flapped them slowly. He was grinning, but he winced as he put a little weight on his bad hip. 'I knew who he was. He lived not far from our house. A few days after his eagle stunt, he came round to ask if he could borrow a quirly-quirly.'

'A *what*?'

'He meant a brace and bit. The wind had blown down a big tree in their garden and he wanted to bore a lot of holes in it. He filled the holes with gunpowder and blew the tree up into little splinters. I got pally with him after that. And with his brother. We called them Trunkie One and Trunkie Two.'

'Didn't know he had a brother. What became of him?'

'Poor devil. He got killed racing at Donnington in '33. He'd got hold of a Velocette that had been used in practice for the TT. It had a defective gearbox. Kept jumping out of top at high speeds. Trunkie One tried to make him have it put right before the race, but he insisted it would be all right. Anyway, during the race, he glanced down at the foot change while he was trying to get in gear. He went off the road, hit a tree, and was flung off. He'd have been unharmed but for the fact that he was wearing a helmet that was too small for him. The helmet was knocked off, and the skin rubbed off his head, right down to the skull. It took him two days to die.'

I shivered, thinking of the rasp of bone, the jagged ends of skin.

'He was always having accidents. I remember seeing him hit a car down Poplar Road. He slid over the roof, and left the lobe of his ear on a wastepaper basket fixed to a lamp-post. We all knew he'd kill himself one day.'

'What about Trunkie One? Did he ever get hurt in races?'

'Everybody did. We all did. Trunkie's got a blue mark in his lip to this day from a cinder that got under the skin when he crashed his bike at Perry Barr. Mind you, he was a good rider. He competed against all the big men of the day. Dirt-track riding had only been in existence for a year or so, but already there were professional riders. There was Sprouts Elder from America, and Vic Huxley, and Daredevil Billy Smythe, and Billy Lamont from Australia. They say that Vic Huxley earned three thousand pounds in six months. That was big money in those days. The big prizes were the Golden Helmet and Golden Gauntlet. Trunkie never stood a chance in the big races. It used to take us half an hour to strip down his bike for a race. The big boys had special machines – speciality bikes that were only meant for racing. Sprouts Elder rode a "Peashooter" Harley-Davidson, and Gentle Jimmy Gent had a Dunelt two-stroke. Jimmy used to drill holes in the flywheel, to make it lighter. One night, I remember, it split and flew out of the crank-case. After the race was over, he walked along and picked up all the pieces and put them in his helmet. Great days, they were, before dirt-track racing became too professional.'

'Sounds like it. Skulls showing through the skin.'

'But they were. Great days. If you'd got a bike, you were better off than a king. You'd come away from a race meeting and fancy yourself as a daredevil rider like Dicky Smythe. Being out of work and poor didn't matter any more. One night, at Hall Green or Perry Barr, Sir Henry Seagrave did a lap of honour. He'd just broken the world speed record in his car, the Golden Arrow. We all imagined that we could do the same on our bikes. It was something to live for. You drew your dole money of fifteen shillings, and for one and fivepence you could have a gallon of petrol and believe you were rolling in money.'

He sat on the bike, sidesaddle, and I took the crutches from him and leaned them against the wall. He unscrewed the cap of the fuel tank, sniffed, and screwed it back on. I tried to imagine what he had looked like when he was nine-

teen years old, when the bike was brand-new. I'd seen photographs of him as a boy and as a man in his twenties, but I
had no picture of him as an adolescent, out of work and
speed-crazy. It pleased me to think that he had used the
bike as an instrument of his dreams in much the same way
I had done. It pleased me to see him sitting sidesaddle on
it, in the attitude of a rider who has made a racing push
start. He was twisting the throttle and testing the clutch and
brake levers, fingering the gear change at the side of the
tank: a boy again, sound in wind and limb.

'Come on,' I said. 'It's about time you were back in the
house. We only came for a quick look. Mum's going to be
back before long.'

'She used to go to the track with me sometimes. We all
had pillion seats. Flapper brackets, we called them. You ask
her if she can remember the tune that was always being
played over the loud-speaker when we first started going to
the race meetings. "My Blue Heaven." You ask her.'

'There'll be hell to pay if she gets home and finds you're
not in. And she'll blame me for putting you up to it.'

'Quite right, too. You did. I'd better start getting the
covers on again.'

'Don't bother to do that. You'll be moving it in a day or
two. I tell you what. I'll keep it round at my place if you
can't find anywhere else. Come on.'

He stood up and took his crutches. When he'd lit his pipe,
he switched off the light and went outside and waited for
me to close and padlock the door. Neither of us spoke on
the way back to the house. I thought of him as a corporal
dispatch rider in the Home Guard during the war, and how
he'd camouflaged the Ariel with brown and green paint. The

bike used to be a tank for me in those days, or a jeep, or an armoured car. When we were sitting down in the living room, I told him about my fantasies on the bike when he wasn't there to see what I was doing. He said he'd give the bike to me one day if I wanted it, but I said I wouldn't dream of taking it away from him.

By the time Mum got home, he was making plans for cleaning up the bike and overhauling the engine during his weeks of recuperation. When his leg was better, perhaps he'd be able to ride it in the Veterans' annual run from London to Brighton. All he'd need to buy was a pair of tyres. He guessed he could do the fastest time of any bike in the race; after all, the day he put it in Mrs Ogden's garage he'd done a comfortable seventy-odd. He was talking fast and excitedly when Mum came in with the shopping.

'What's come over *you* all of a sudden?' she said.

'Ask her,' he said. 'Ask her what tune they used to play.'

THE CREMATION

The phone rang. I picked it up before the dog began to bark, and gave my number.

'That you, John?'

'Hello, Dad. What's the weather like your end?' He's only twenty-five miles along the coast, but we always compare climates.

'Bit blowy. You were quick. Expecting a call?'

'Didn't want the dog to start barking. Got a dog. Collected him yesterday from the kennels. Name of Sam. Got him on approval for a week. Take him back Wednesday if he don't suit.'

'Cross between a hedgehog and a grindstone, daresay?'

'Border collie, mainly. What's new? Car still OK, I hope. You don't want any more trouble with that gearbox.' I lit a cigarette and pulled over an ashtray. I could hear my father lighting his pipe. His TV was on, the sound turned low. It was the news.

'Turn it up a bit,' I said. 'I want to hear whether they've caught that killer.' But then I heard the music being played that follows the bulletin. My clock must have been slow. The dog had settled down again by the fire. He was going to be all right.

'They've not caught him. That other chap – the ex-copper – died this afternoon in hospital. Know who it was?'

'No. Do you, then?'

'Yes. Old Arthur.'

'You mean old Arthur who –'

'That's him. Still got that helmet somewhere he gave you when you were a nipper. Poor old Arthur. Christ! Fine thing when your schoolmates get shot in the stomach. Jenny phoned to let me know. They came down to see me, not above five or six weeks ago. Who'd have thought it, eh? Can't take it in. Jenny wondered whether I'd go to the funeral. But I don't know. Birmingham's a long way, this weather, and the car's still playing up a bit. What's it like your end?'

'The same. Forecast says snow tonight – drifting, if this wind doesn't give over. When's the funeral? Bit soon to know yet, daresay. Sorry about your old mate, Dad.'

'They'll have him. Two policemen dead? They'll have every man available out with dogs. Jenny thinks Wednesday or Thursday. She'll be letting me know. I suppose I could go up on the train. I ought to go. Don't really want to, but there it is. He's going to be cremated. I don't like the idea of cremations. Never been to one myself. Seems all wrong to me.'

'Same here. Had to go to one once – one of my pupils. Only thirteen, he was. All through the term he came to school, never absent. We could see he was dying; got whiter and whiter. This time of year it was. He died just as we'd got used to him being there every day. I used to correct his homework just as if –'

'Remember you telling me. Funny thing, you had a new dog then, didn't you? Hope you have better luck with this one. Is it behaving itself?'

'Very good, so far. Look, Dad, I don't go back to work until Friday. Why not let me drive you up? You don't want to be bothered with trains, having to cross London and wait about at Paddington. Never mind the snow. We start early, take it gently, be more certain to get you there on time than if you went by train. Anyway, the snow might have cleared by then. I've got a pair of new tyres on the back wheels and I've had the heater repaired. Do it in comfort. If the service is in the afternoon, let's see . . . say five hours' drive should do it. Leave at seven, do it easily.'

'Jenny said the afternoon. Wednesday or Thursday. Nice of you to offer. Can you spare the time, though? Didn't you say you had to go and see about the dog Wednesday? I don't want to go, honest I don't. But what can I do? I'd have to catch the six-seventeen from here. If the funeral's not over before half-past three, I wouldn't be able to get back the same day. That'd mean – '

'Dad – '

'No, I'll not bother. The weather's bound to be ribby. Old Arthur won't know, one way or the other. He thought the world of you, you know.'

'Got to go, Dad. Somebody at the door. Give us a bell when you know which day, and I'll pick you up. I'm really sorry, Dad. He was a good bloke. Don't worry, I'll get you there. Goodnight.'

'Ah. Goodnight.'

There was nobody at the door. I took Sam for a walk in the snow. By the time we got back, our prints had been refilled.

Wednesday it was. I got up in the dark. When I left, the sun was rising on another new fall of snow: pink, or blue, according to whether you looked into the light or away from it. It lay deep along the beach, and the windless, frozen sea lay dirty and still all along it. I whistled the dog and put him in the back of the car, where he shook himself and lay quiet. The heater whined as I drove down the empty coast road. The gritters had been at work, leaving a trail of yellow and tired, impacted ice. My father was waiting at his gate, holding a rough bunch of large-bloomed chrysanthemums and a blue canvas bag.

'We can't go in this,' he said. 'There'll be ten-foot drifts up-country.'

'Nah. They'll have cleared the main roads. So long as we keep going gently, we'll be all right. Say hello to Sam.'

He put the flowers and the bag in the front and leaned over to stroke the dog. He looked chilled; his cheeks were sunken, as though he'd had all his teeth out. When I started the engine, he turned round in the seat and slammed the door.

For the first twenty miles, he wouldn't talk. I noticed how his right foot pressed down as we approached corners; I couldn't see his foot, but I could hear the paper wrapping round the flowers crinkle as he pumped an imaginary brake.

'When you were little,' I said, 'did you stand at the front of a tram and pretend to be the driver?'

He grinned and picked up the flowers and put them in the back. 'If that black-hearted limb of Satan chews up old Arthur's flowers, I'll wring his neck. Sorry. I've never been a good passenger. Look at those ducks on the ice.'

'Geese.'

'Geese, ah. Could do with a hot drink. How about you?'

'Ought to keep going. Hundred and thirty miles yet.'

'Papers reckon they'll catch him by the weekend. The

snow's hampering them. Dogs can't work if the scent's smothered up.'

'They've started dropping hay bales from helicopters.'

'Be for the cattle.'

'I know.'

'Cattle won't dig down for food like sheep.'

'I know.'

'If old Arthur had been shot after the snow fell, they'd have caught that swine. Dogs won't dig for the scent – or can't.'

'You sure? Sam dug something out of the snow on the beach this morning. Some scrap. Somebody had a fire there last night. Bits of black wood half burned and a hole in the snow. Kids had a barbecue, daresay. Anyway, Sam found something to eat.'

'Fresh though, see? No hopes, after a day or two.'

'Let's stop and have a shiver. Made good time, not a skid.'

He'd brought a thermos of coffee and some rough-hewn cheese sandwiches. I let Sam out for a pee.

It was the top of a hill. A row of trees looked stunted, sucked down in a drift. There were cows standing still behind their breath. I thought for a moment that it was beginning to snow again, but it was only a few flakes dislodged by a crow in the tree by us.

'Want to drive?'

'No, you drive.'

'We'll have to keep going now till we get there. Don't like the look of the sky up north.'

'Still turn back, if you'd rather. It's always two overcoats colder in Brum. Wouldn't matter to me. I'm not keen on burials.'

'Cremations, Dad.'

'Nor them. Come on, you could turn round before we cross the Thames. No harm done. Been a nice drive.'

'No. I'm going to get you there. You ought to go. Be glad, once you're there.'

'Don't be too sure.'

'Have a kip. Give you the nudge when we're in Warwickshire.'

But I was surprised when he slumped down and slept. As soon as I was certain he was well away, I went faster on straight stretches. He stirred now and again when I slowed down or stopped in thick traffic, but he didn't wake up. My eyes were tired from the glare of new snow. As we entered Stratford, I shook him. 'Remove your hat for Shakespeare,' I said. But by the time he'd come to, the statue was left behind. He looked out as we were passing a newsagent's. I stopped and bought a first edition of the evening paper. The front page was full of a train derailment; but there it was in the stop-press. 'Police Killer Captured Near Redditch. Funeral of Retired Detective Sergeant 2.30 This Afternoon, Lodge Hill Crematorium.'

The last few miles, he pointed out places on the road that had memories for him. I wouldn't say 'I know,' although I knew, from countless similar journeys in the past, the spot where he'd crashed his motorbike when he was seventeen, the house where, as an apprentice, he'd hung his first door, the lane where he'd had his first smoke. Then, 'That's the police station where old Arthur began,' he said. 'I didn't know,' I said. I didn't know.

'I ever tell you I tried to get into the police? Start of the Depression. Had to do a test. One of the first questions –'

'Was: "Have you had a university education?"'

'Ah. And we had to do a dictation.'

'And the man was a Glaswegian, and you couldn't under-stand half he said. So you failed.'

'I wasn't good enough.'

He'd never said that before. 'So you went south, and that's where I got born.'

'If I'd been as clever as Arthur, you'd have been born a Midlander.'

'There's a thought.'

'Lots of things would've been different, mebbe.'

'Glad the man was from Glasgow.'

'Might have got in nowadays. They could pick and choose then. Still – look what became of old Arthur. Third on the right now, number thirty-five. Coming in?'

I stopped the car, left the engine running.

'Not dressed for it. Anyway, they'll have a houseful.'

'I'll have to. Look, the curtains are drawn. He's at home, then. In that front room, I bet, where his old man used to read the racing papers. I remember when *he* went. *He* lay in that front room. Expect Arthur'll have a flag over his coffin. Shall I take the flowers in? Better. I'll be out soon as I can. Sit in the car with you until the procession moves off. Must have a word with Jenny. Dunno know what to say, though. What *can* you say? You could turn the car round while I'm inside. Lodge Hill's back the way we came. Up on a hill, it is. Cold as charity.'

As he went up to the door, I moved off to turn the car round. He was holding the flowers behind his back. He'd always been ashamed of holding flowers. Behind me, the dog began to whine. He was still whining after I'd put on the hand-brake and turned the key. Cars were arriving, doors slamming. There was a line of cones outside the house, which I ignored. All along the terrace of houses, windows were being opened, dislodging snow from sills. A crowd was gathering on the pavement. There were several policemen in their best uniforms, carrying wreaths. One of them tapped my window, asked if I was one of the mourners. 'Sort of,' I said, and explained about my Dad, who was now coming out of the front door. 'Do you want us to move?' I asked. 'No, sir. As long as there's room for the hearse, and I think there is.' And the policeman walked away, pulling his gloves back on.

Dad got into the car. 'Many in there?' I said.

'Don't know most of 'em. Said hello to Jenny. Crying, you might know. Better off out here. He *is* in there. Didn't go and look. Somebody said. Look at these crowds. Might have guessed. They'll all turn out. His son's not here, though. In Belgium. Couldn't make it, he said.'

'Could've been here quicker than it took us to drive.'

'Never did like him.'

The hearse arrived, and four more large, black, empty cars. The fourth one couldn't get into the space in front of me. There was a yard or two to spare behind my car. I started to reverse to make room; but already the coffin, draped in the Union Flag, was being carried out. I stopped. Dad hadn't seen what was happening, and opened his door to help me reverse. When he saw the coffin, he kept quite still, one leg out of the car, the door wide open. I wouldn't shift the gear lever into neutral until the coffin had been placed in the hearse and an abundance of flowers placed on top. I saw Dad's chrysanthemums being carried out. My leg ached with the cold from the open door and the pressure of the clutch pedal. The engine cut out, but I kept my foot down. The four big cars filled, and one by one moved off. Dad sat back in his seat and closed his door; and I re-started the engine and followed the procession. There were other cars behind us, ever so many. All the way to the crematorium there were crowds lining the streets. Traffic was held up, or stopped of its own accord, to let us through. We didn't go fast enough for third gear, and the engine sounded too busy and irreverent in second. 'Funny thing was,' my Dad said, 'Arthur never was much cop at spelling.' He said this when we were outside the crematorium. The front cars had already emptied. We were used by now to the crowds, the black uniforms. A guard of honour had lined up at the door. Frail snow was falling on them. High-ranking police officers were going into the chapel, smoothing grey hair as they removed their caps.

'I'm only going in if you come with me. I never know when you're supposed to kneel. Where do you sit? All these important people. Will there be special seats for friends of the family?'

'I'll come with you. Keep your coat on. It'll be draughty inside. Always is, in these places.'

We got out of the car, and I locked all the doors. As we walked past the guard of honour – at ease, now – we could hear the dog whining. In the porch, as we caught sight of the draped coffin on its catafalque, and the formal lilies arranged in tall brass vases, he began to bark. Many of the congregation turned round toward the west window, away from the coffin. As we hesitated, the barking became more powerful – dry, hard and regular. I noticed people who had been outside with us, now in the seats I had been making for. The chapel was full to overflowing. The organ was playing; the throb and shudder of its lower notes vibrated; but the dog's barking was even louder, and it was not going to stop.

'I'll have to go out and keep him quiet,' I whispered. 'Can't let him carry on like this. Not right.'

'I'll come with you. There's nowhere for me.'

It took us a few minutes to calm the dog. He'd been abandoned by his previous owners. 'It's all right, Sam,' I told him. My Dad has never liked dogs, but he let Sam lick his face all over. The closed windows steamed up and we sat listening to a hymn being sung. When Sam sat up on my lap, he wagged his tail, wiping part of the windscreen clear. Outside the chapel door, the undertaker's men were finishing their cigarettes, flicking their stubs into the snow. The hearse driver tossed flowers from the back of his vehicle on to the ground, slammed the tailgate door, then drove away fast. The hymn finished.

'What do they do with our flowers?' Dad said. 'I thought they'd have been burned with him. Look at them, thrown anyhow on the ground.'

'Hospitals have them. Old-folks' homes. Not wasted.'

'What's going on inside now? It's all gone quiet. I suppose when everybody comes out, they'll take him away and just burn him.'

I told him how the coffin moves forward on mechanical rollers and disappears through little swing doors behind the altar; and how the little doors shut, and that's the last you see.

'Then what?'

'Dunno. Boiler room behind, or something. See that tower with louvres at the top? Expect that's where they let out –'

'There were good brass handles on the coffin. Saw them when the flag nearly fell off outside the house. Do they pick them out of the ashes when it's cool enough?'

'Don't think about it, Dad. Remember Arthur how he was.'

'Ah. Best thing. And best be going now, before they all come out. Be getting dark. Been a wasted journey in a way. For you, I mean. Brought me all this way.'

'I'm glad I brought the dog.'

'Same here. Nice, ain't he? Lot of collie in him. Very protective, collies are. He didn't want us near all them policemen, eh?'

I started the engine.

'Trouble with dogs,' he said, 'when they die it's very upsetting. They always die. Get run over, get too old.'

I turned the headlights on as we left the city. It was distinctly warmer and the snow was melting fast. The journey back wouldn't take too long.

'You can always get another one,' I said, 'a little while later.' He turned and looked at me. 'A dog,' I said. 'Another dog.'

'Not the same,' he said. 'Never the same. You only remember the first one.'

Soon it was utterly dark. He cradled the dog and fell silent. I turned the radio on loud so that he could think on his own. The farther south we went, the more frequently we passed the blazing lights of greenhouses where chrysanthemums are grown through the winter. You can always buy chrysanthemums. I turned to him to ask if he wanted to stop for a hot drink, but he was asleep. He was beginning to look really old, I thought, and I must find a way of letting him know that I wouldn't forget his views about cremation.

THE LOFT

It was in his pigeon-loft that I found my Dad. I was pressing my forehead against the wire mesh, trying to adjust my eyes to the penumbra of the loft after the harsh brass of mid-afternoon sun, when I became aware of him. He was sprawled in that bleached and crud-spattered Windsor chair of his, his cap pulled hard down over his eyes as usual. His big carpenter's hands were cradling, with stiff fingers interlaced, a pure-white fantail pigeon. He was utterly still. I counted slowly to ten. There was no sign of his breathing. I counted to ten once more. There wasn't a movement in the pigeon-loft: not a flutter among the hundred birds, not a flicker of my Dad's eyelids. I'd seen bronze, life-size statues looking more alive than he did. There's one near Circular Quay in Sydney: a man on a bench, reading a newspaper; and you'd swear he was about to turn the page. But my Dad was not about to release that pigeon back into its cage. He was dead. My God, my Dad was dead.

I had believed, ever since my Mum died, that this was how he'd finish up – at peace, in his pigeon-loft, comfortably, in that old Windsor chair that had been my grandma's. It was how he'd have wanted to go. It was how my Mum would have wanted him to go. I noticed how a paper sack of feed had fallen to the ground beside him. It had split, and the corn had spilled along the slabs under the nest-boxes. Strange, I thought: not like my Dad to sit down and relax before sweeping up.

Strange, too, what comes to mind in the first, dumbfounded moments of bereavement, before you're ready for the first ordeals of grief. When Mum went I thought, *She'll never get that bit of knitting finished*; and now, in this instant, I was staring at half a pound of spilt kibbled maize. Immediately, as had happened at Mum's bedside in the hospital, I knew precisely how much, and in what ways, I had loved and revered this parent of mine; how, from now on, I was set at liberty from his influence. *No man is free until his father dies*, someone has written; and the aphorism returned to me as it often had done over the years.

The pigeon he was clutching on his lap was tranquil, its tail spread wide and elegantly behind my Dad's fingers. Its sinuous neck rested like an offcut of silken white cord over his crossed thumbs. It cocked its head this way and that, from unflurried curiosity; but when I involuntarily coughed – from an onrush of shock, as well from as the warm, amoniac vapours of the loft – a disturbed flurry of worried cooing rippled through all the birds in their compartments. I shuddered at the thought of having to touch my Dad. We had always avoided touching. Even a handshake had to be got over in a brusque instant of mutual discomfiture. But also I had always loathed the feel of birds, their otherness: something to do with their smoothened feathers and the racing palpitations those feathers enclosed. My first act of defiance, as a boy, was when I refused ever again to go into the loft. I would not, I said, no matter what. The old chap affected to believe it was the smell I objected to. 'It's the stink as turns the lad's stomach,' he told some crony of his as I slunk from the loft and away through the garden gate. But Dad wasn't daft: he sensed what sickened me. He accepted that I couldn't be doing with his fantails and tumblers and the reeking loft where, at night, I knew how they huddled and clung with their scaly feet. Like my mother, I would hence-forth refuse to stroke a favorite bird if, on the lawn of a Sunday morning, he proffered it to me before kissing its head and tossing it heavenwards to fly, briefly free.

I looked again through the mesh. Dad's whole frame, broad chest taut in his jersey as flour in a sack, size eleven feet in hobnailed boots, might have been cast in bronze. Never mind what I'd felt in the past: surely I ought to steel myself, enter the loft, take hold of him, lay him out seemly among the bright yellow spillings of corn. A good son should effect that act of homage. But no – I wasn't up to prising hands and fingers in *rigor mortis* from a live bird which would then fly frantically about in the confined space of the loft. There were special people whose job this was. When Mum died, Dad had been content for a WVS lady to dispose of her clothes. He could no more have gone through Mum's things than desecrate a shrine.

So I went into the house to decide what to do – telephone, call on a neighbour or whatever. But first, I needed a long drink of cold water. The glasses were still unaccountably kept out of sight, behind the television. I went to the fridge on the slim off-chance of finding some ice-cubes – Dad wasn't the sort to have much use for ice – but found it imposs-ible to open the freezer compartment. I banged it with the ball of my thumb, then with my fist. I stood, stupidly impotent, staring at the giveaway chunky tumbler that Dad, now stock-still among his pigeons, had acquired one day at a filling-station. It was the discovery of this, the icing-up of his freezer compartment, that prompted my tears. I should have offered to defrost it for him. Not that he'd have let me.

Since Mum died, I'd taken to visiting him two, sometimes three, times a month, always on Saturdays and always for no longer than a bare two hours. I'd arrive mid-afternoon and leave before early evening: that way we weren't obliged to eat a meal together, which suited him. Restaurants for him were out of the question on account of class-consciousness and hygiene even more than expense – 'There's not one of them snooty places but the kitchen's filthy, you mark my words,' he'd say. Eating at my house was out of the question because he wouldn't countenance my driving for an hour to pick him up and another to take him home – to say nothing of his witnessing *a son of mine pithering about in an apron.* Moreover, we could never have shared so much as a snack in that old-fashioned kitchen no longer my mother's: for him to prepare a simple sandwich in front of me, and for me, would have been an intolerable embarrassment to him. I'd not discovered what he'd learned about cooking or shopping. He'd been taking good enough care of himself until now, I'd had to suppose, always looking well and robust. He'd neither gained nor lost any weight and his complexion was ruddily healthy.

Maybe he made do with wholesome fare requiring little preparation – a crusty loaf, a raw onion and a hunk of cheese, followed by a couple of rosy apples, all painstakingly sculpted into geometrically precise morsels with the bone-handled penknife my great-grandfather had given him on his thirteenth birthday. But where did these simple commodities come from? Dad was independent and proud as well as frugal; suspicious of strangers as a primitive tribesman, aloof from neighbours, he wouldn't let anyone perform domestic chores for him. 'Listen here to me. Say this once and I won't have it mentioning again. I'll not have any truck with scheming widow-women coming round, thinking as they can get their feet under *my* table,' he said to me, the day after Mum's funeral. I'd suggested he advertise for a home-help to come round a few hours a week to clean and take care of his laundry and shopping. 'What do I care about things like that, now that your Ma's gone?' By *things like that* maybe he'd assumed I'd been hinting at comforts other than a newly-ironed shirt, a room hoovered and dusted and a fridge full of provisions. I was grieved to think he could have judged me guilty of what would have been, to him, a gross impropriety. All I'd intended was to show concern for him in his new, bafflingly lonely situation; for now he'd have to fend for himself and attend to domestic tasks he'd taken for granted all his life. I knew: I'd been through all that. Now he'd have to find out what was kept in which drawer or cupboard; now he'd find his bed unmade and he'd wonder why the kitchen sink no longer smelt sweet. He'd have to learn the mysteries of supermarkets, for surely he'd soon tire of a peasant's diet and yearn for the kind of properly cooked, properly balanced meals my Mum had set before him.

Not during my growing up, or during the rest of my Mum's lifetime, or since, had I ever once seen him with so much as a frying pan in his hand, let alone a basket of groceries. He'd make himself a brew of strong tea sometimes; and I remember how, in the days before families like ours ran to a fridge, he'd stand a long while at the open larder door, contemplating the cold and angular remains of our half shoulder of lamb or the scraggy carcass of a chicken before, and as if reluctantly, persuading away a sliver of fat or frizzled skin for an impromptu, miniature snack. But, 'Would I expect your Ma to hammer floors or take a ripsaw to a pitchpine board?' he'd have demanded, had anyone suggested he cook dinner if – and this was thankfully seldom – my Mum fell poorly. As a boy, I had sometimes had to forage like a pygmy.

So these days, whenever I arrived at the house where I was born, and stepped inside the back door and called a greeting to announce my presence, it was always to find every one of the blue, chipped enamel pots and pans not in use but ranged as ever along the shelves where my mother had ordained them to be kept since years before she had been pregnant with me; and there was never a stray plate or fork in what was called 'the middle room.' Here my father would usually be, reading the paper, smoking his pipe, with everything in perfect order, thoroughly prepared for my arrival: never in the garden; and certainly never (acknowledging my dislike of his precious pigeons) in the loft. He'd have been none the wiser, had I ever crept in very quietly and not shouted my 'Hello, Dad,' but instead satisfied a harmless nosiness by opening the odd cupboard door or rummaging about in certain drawers on my way through. However in our family, being trusted not to pry (or *brevitt*, my father's word) was a strict conditioning of childhood: I could no more have sneaked open the door of his fridge to find out what he'd got for dinner than I could once have peeked through keyholes at my mother's unthinkable nakedness.

Somehow we'd fixed upon two hours – and not two hours of the busy morning – as a reasonable duration for a visit, three weeks out of four. Maybe six hours a month – that's all I spent with my widower father. He'd never suggested I should go more frequently or for longer at a time. Two hours

was time enough for us to keep easy and companionable:
not enough for there to be longueurs amid the commonplace
things that forever needed saying. Enough for us to sidle
towards the great philosophical themes of love and death
and religion: nowhere near enough to begin to expand upon
them or to give ourselves away to each other. Our two hours
were precisely what he had come to expect of me; and at
his age, and considering his apparently unrelieved solitar-
iness, they were paradoxically too long *and* too short for
there not to be some trace of regret, on both his part and
mine, when I got up and peremptorily clasped his hand. In
that abrupt moment he would, with an unwonted flicker of
his steady eye, readily acknowledge that another of my visits
was at an end and that neither of us knew whether there
would be an interval of one week or two before the next.
Our parting words and gestures had become ritualised, which
neither of us minded. Just once, after the handshake, he had
gripped my left shoulder in his right hand, squeezing hard
enough to signal his father's love but not quite hard enough
for me to be affected by it until I was a mile or two into my
journey. 'You're getting grey as a badger,' he had said as a
parting shot on one occasion; and, on another, 'When you
was knee-high to a grasshopper, you used to sing all them
songs your Ma taught you. Liked that, I did.'

Sometimes I'd leave, believing that next time he might
pour out his heart. He never would now. He'd left it too
late.

I drank a glass of tepid water from the tap, then decided
to phone his doctor. My face was taut with drying tears. I
washed it and dabbed it dry with a tea-towel; then went to
the 'middle room.' I'd never seen it in such a mess as it was
in.

In the drawer of the telephone table I found his address book. His doctor's name was, I knew, McCallan, but I found the number in the D's. I got a recorded message saying where the doctor might be reached at which hours of the day and night. I hung up and began to jot down the complicated information on the back of a letter, on pink writing-paper, which had fallen from the address book. I was about to write down the second of the numbers when I heard the rattle of the back door latch. One of his neighbours, I thought; or, more likely, one of his pigeon-fancying mates from the club. I was glad to have someone – anyone – to be with me. I stood up to welcome whoever it was.

But it was my father who came into the room, lumbering and sleepy. And I startled him no less than he startled me. The instant he recognised me, he became alert and on the offensive.

'Thought you was a burglar,' he said. 'This ain't your week to come. You was here last week *and* the week before that. You never come three weeks on the trot. Look at the state I'm in.'

I was appalled at his being alive. I stared at his being. He was breathing heavily, and he glowered. He'd brought the smell of the pigeon-loft indoors with him. It filled the room with pungency. Wisps of downy feather adhered to his jacket. He was right. Of course he was right. It was the third success-ive week of visits. I couldn't account for my mistake.

'Well, Dad . . .' I began. But I found nothing more to say. I just shrugged, a little boy caught red-handed.

'And hey-up, mister – what d'you think you've been a-bre-vitting after?' he said, in the tungsten voice he'd not used on me since I was an adolescent. 'You can just hand over that there here.' He snatched the pink letter from my hand

and stuffed it in his pocket. 'You have no right, poking about in my stuff.'

I felt as though I was choking on a lump of flint.

'Oh my God, Dad!' I managed to say. 'I thought –'

'Never mind about God and I *thought*. No right, I say.'

'No – but I was just –'

'I know what you was *just*. But none o' my private letters got nowt to do wi' *you*. So just you think on.'

*

THINK on I did, through our difficult two hours that afternoon; and during my drive back home; and continually throughout the two weeks that have elapsed since. I've not felt up to phoning him, and he hasn't phoned me. Tomorrow I must go to see him. I'll find him in the 'middle room' as usual. Perhaps he'll expect me to give an account of myself; perhaps, on the other hand, he will choose not to allude to my unexpected visit or to that letter on pink writing paper. *Pink.* I don't know how I'd be able to say I hadn't read it. I don't know how I'd be able to say that I'd thought he'd died.

I've speculated, of course, about the identity of the writer of that letter, and the nature of its contents. If ever my Dad decides to tell me that there's a lady in his life, he'll have to devise a way for us to talk about her. Then there'd be the awkward business of my meeting her. He'll have to find a way round that, too. What *I* have to find a way round is ridding myself of the image which obsesses me night and day: that of how my Dad must have looked at the moment before his coming back from the dead in the pigeon-loft. How that snow-white bird in his encircling fingers might

have wriggled, rousing him. How it might have crawled from
his lap towards his chest and then have flown up from him,
like the soul leaving the body in the engraving hanging in
the 'middle room', that had once been great-grandma's.

SCENES IN A COUNTRY CHURCHYARD

Soon after I brought my family to live in this village – getting on for thirty years ago now – my father came, unexpectedly and on his own, to visit. He'd already inspected the house before the exchange of contracts: had dug his shiny, pocket-worn penknife into woodwork, testing for rot; had sniffed for damp. The old place would see me out, he'd said. Sound oak sills and frames; no damp-course, but the walls were good and thick.

'Come on,' I said, before he could take his coat off, 'I want to take you down to see the church and the church-yard.'

Farmyard, I'd meant to say; but I let it go.

'Morbid blighter,' he said. But he grinned, doing up his top button again. I grinned back at him. He was in his mid-fifties, and I was just turned thirty. He had grown into an unexpected handsomeness, having filled out at last into his face and his frame. Nowadays we were sometimes taken for brothers, which pleased us both: I had matured, and he was not yet beginning to look old. Death for us was that which happened to other people.

'Sally's taken the kids shopping,' I said. 'Be home when we get back. Have ourselves a cup of tea then. No Mum?'

'Women's Institute meeting, or summat. What about your coat?'

'Mneh.'

But the wind off the coast struck cold across the meadows as we strolled down Church Lane. Augusts can sometimes feel wintry, even south of the Downs. Surreptitiously, I turned up the collar of my jacket.

'What'd I tell you?' he said. 'Never listen.'

'How d'you like this lane, then? Pure Sussex. Unspoiled.'

And indeed the lane was still lovely in those days. The line of summer-dusted ancient elms had not yet been ravaged by the Dutch disease; no bungalows in-filling between the thatch-and-flint cottages; the pub still stood in its wilderness of a garden; cows rested their chops in gaps of the hawthorn hedge, drooling their long, pink spittles.

'Not a bad second-best,' he said – as I knew he would. Dad was a Warwickshire man. He'd lost nothing of his midlands accent. I'd been born in Sussex only because he and my mother had had to move south during the thirties, in search of a job for him.

'Own up,' I said. 'You'd never go back to Brummagem, would you?'

He had us stop and lean on a five-barred gate. He scraped the dottle from his pipe, filled it with dark shag, tamped it down, flicked his much-pocked Zippo lighter on the ball of his thumb, ignited the top shreds of tobacco, tamped again, flicked again, ignited again, furiously puffed, finally put the lighter away, before grudgingly allowing that, no, he wouldn't ever want to go back. Not now.

'Nobody left, see?' he said. I'd lit a cigarette. 'And you ought to knock off them damn coffin-nails, and all.'

'Daresay.'

To reach our church, you have to pass through the farm-yard. I wanted Dad to see the medieval tithe barn propped up on its mushroom-shaped steddles, to catch a whiff of cowdung from the cobbled midden outside the milking-parlour. When I'd been a little boy, he'd taken me to see the village where his father had grown up – but which he'd had to leave in order to seek work in the city. I'd been led through a similar, centuries-old farmyard, with a similar, pervading reek. The land up there in his home territory ploughed up oppressive red; down here the earth's a restful café-au-lait, what with the chalky sub-soil. I could never feel at home where he grew up. Even as a child, taken on visits, I'd noticed how the bricks of the police-house where he'd been born had baked to a different tone and texture from those I was used to. Besides, up there you're as far as you can ever be in England from the sea, and there's no tang of salt in the air; I would stifle. Dad had never glimpsed the sea until that day in 1933 when he halted, and propped his motorbike on its stand on the crest of the South Downs, and surveyed the English Channel, the ribbon-development of towns along the coast road, and wondered whether he might get a start rough-carpentering somewhere there below, among the hideous, jerry-built, speculative sites. I suppose he thought he'd not stop long: but stop here he did.

Just inside the churchyard, once you've paused under the pitched roof of the lych-gate, you pass the horrifically cracked-open chest-tombs of families who had lived in my house since the time of Queen Anne: the Collinses, the Bonifaces. If you cared to, you might peer between the fissures and maybe see their very bones.

'Nice lettering,' he said, bending over to squint at some elegant, eighteenth-century, deep-chiselled inscriptions.

'Hope they don't get out and come and haunt you. Still their house, in a way. That's how they'd think of it. You've not had time to mek it yours yet. Not properly. Teks time, with old houses.'

'Don't you start. We've been told we've got a ghost.'

'Oh ah?'

'According to the old couple who keep the shop.'

'So what d'you mek of it?'

'Barn owl in the attic, most like. There's mice and all sorts scuttling about up there. Nest in the thatch, daresay.'

'You want to get summat done about it, mister, whatever it is. Before it gets damn sight wuss. Might drive you out, else. Has been known. Ah, mark my words.'

'Nothing's likely to get *me* on the move again, Dad,' I said. 'I'm staying here for good. I'm settled. Staying put. I've got what I want. Nice old house, two kids, good job. Know what I mean?' I'd wanted to get this said to him, and to have his approval. He was a great one for stability and security.

'What does your Sally think? She dain't seem to go on it much.'

'She'll get to like it more, give her time.'

'Not good, having no proper tradesmen's entrance, though. Kids traipsing mud through your front door everlasting. I can see her point of view.'

We followed the path past the church porch. I showed him the brick and tile rubble in the south wall of the chancel, which had been scavenged from the remains of a Roman villa a few hundred yards away. We reached the beech hedge that separated the old part of the churchyard from the new, and walked beyond it to the plot of recent graves. There remained an ample, tapering parcel of ground in those days, when my Dad was younger than I am now. Its boundary was marked with a barbed-wire fence, beyond which there stretched fields of wheat and barley; and, beyond them, the railway line. Beyond that still, there were more fields of cereals, and fields of peas and beans, until, just further off than the eye could see into the sea-fret, there extended the coast.

My Dad inspected the dates on a new tombstone. Then, beginning with his calves pressed against the back of it, he paced away, about thirty steps, into the yet untroubled rough grass which terminated at the compost mound, where mourners dumped their mowings and spent flowers. He stopped and turned and faced me.

'Reckon you'll get popped in just about here,' he said, 'when your time comes.' He dug his heel into the turf, the way a rugby player prepares for placing the ball before a penalty kick.

'Now who's a morbid blighter?' I said. All he did was laugh; but I knew how I would always remember the exact spot where his heel had gone in – seven fence-posts along one way: dead in line with the edge of the church tower, the other. In my mind's eye I saw the first sod being turned by the spade. There'd be silverweed and buttercups in it.

'Tek no notice o' me,' he said. 'Be no room left at all by the time it's your turn. They'll have got well into them corn fields by then.'

I wasn't best pleased when the couple in the village shop insisted, within hearing of our daughters, that our house did indeed contain a ghost. Something of a conventional, commonplace kind of ghost, as it seemed to me: a White

Lady, they said, who appeared at midnight on Christmas Eve. Our girls, then aged eight and nine, shared the bedroom through whose walls the lady passed.

'But there's no need to be afraid,' the old busybodies said. 'She means no harm, and she won't take any notice of you. And she don't hang about – leastways, so folks say.' Sally and I decided never to allude to the subject.

Just before our first New Year here, my parents came over for lunch. In the late afternoon, we all went for a walk down to the farmyard to see the Christmas crib in the tithe barn. The ancient building, its great oak doors unwontedly thrown open, had been transformed into an impromptu rustic theatre containing the familiar tableau of painted plaster figures among the straw. As we approached through the beginnings of dusk, some cleverly concealed lights came on inside the barn: unnerving for an instant, but then poignant in their tender revelation of the unchanging mystery. There was a dusting of snow underfoot, and frost had formed on the weather side of timbers. The Friesians were being released from the milking-parlour, lowing and occasionally bellowing on their way back to the stalls. Wind from off the sea disturbed a few wisps of straw around the crib, and a little chaff flew. You would have sworn that it was the figures that moved; a magical illusion – we all agreed on that. I was not, still am not, a believer, but I've always been vulnerable to the sentimentality of Christmas. It doesn't do much harm to go along with the comfortable myths once a year.

Sally and my Mum said they felt cold, and that they ought to take the girls back home before they got too chilled.

'We'll catch you up,' my Dad said.

He took hold of my elbow and led me a few steps towards the lych-gate.

'Saw that ghost of yours Christmas Eve, did you?' he said quietly.

'Course not. Load of tosh.'

'Ah. Course it's a load of tosh. Still . . .'

'Still what?'

'Bet you wouldn't sit among them chest-tombs now it's dark.' He lifted the Norfolk latch of the gate and rattled it.

'Bet you wouldn't, either.'

'Too right I wouldn't, laddie. I mean – you never can tell, can you?' He rattled the latch again, more gently. He was lost in recollection. 'Ha!' he said.

'What?'

'Your grandfather once dared me to do summat similar. It was after the Harvest Supper. "Go and sit till midnight on the bench in the church porch," he said, "and you can tek a jug o' cider to keep you company." That was summat, and all, jug o' cider, 'cos I was only twelve or thirteen. "No fear," I said, "not me." I dain't dare, see? But *he* would've done, he said. Ah, and he did, and all.'

'What – you mean he really *did* believe it was all a load of tosh?'

'No. Far from it. That's why he wun't afraid, see? That's what I'm saying.'

'I can't remember much about my granddad.'

'Why I'm telling you now. These things need passing on, like, one generation to the next. You'd have liked your granddad. I often think about him, you know.'

And I suppose my daughters often remember *their* granddad, now that he's dead, and now that they've grown up into women with children of their own. What they'll remember best, perhaps, is how he looked on those winter Saturday afternoons when we all went on our ritual walk round the village after lunch. We must have gone on those walks in spring, summer and autumn, too, of course: but if their memories are anything like mine, my girls will bring him back to mind wearing that shabby old car-coat of his, and the tartan muffler, and the flat cap whose brim had long since grown soiled and threadbare. So he looked when we all kicked a football about in the recreation ground, and when he and I shared the see-saw in the playground; also, then, down at the farmyard, when we watched the cows amble stiff-legged, wreathed in warmish steam, from the stalls to the milking-parlour and back again from the milking-parlour to the stalls. Dad's breath, too, whether or not mixed with pipe-smoke, made brief, billowing clouds in the icy air – 'Like the bubbles in a strip-cartoon,' Sally once said, to make us laugh. And my Mum said a strange thing. 'He breathes more in and more out than most folks, your granddad,' she said. She had a way of coming out with off-beat statements like that. We all turned towards her, but she wouldn't be drawn to say more.

Sometimes, fracturing the ritual, we'd go to the farmyard first. In the earlier afternoons, before the start of dusk, before milking-time, there might be a wedding going on in the church. Sally, my Mum and my daughters liked to stand outside the lych-gate, waiting to see the bride in all her billowing white finery, the bridesmaids, the confetti flying. Dad and I would mooch off towards the midden for a smoke until the wedding-party cars were leaving. We would peer through stout, steel bars enclosing the brick-built quarters of the monstrous stud bull, of which we seldom glimpsed more than a hefty head, tough-looking as teak, the ring in its flared, glistening nostrils as big as a quoit. We would stand there, not speaking, or perhaps whispering, as we listened for occasional stirrings in the inner dark of the byre. I found not distasteful the ammoniac whiffs that overlaid the fragrance of our tobacco. I said as much once, and my Dad agreed with me.

Sometimes, though, as we approached along Church Lane, we'd see that there was a funeral going on. We'd glimpse the hearse, the limousines and the out-of-place red and blue and yellow cars of mourners; and we'd not go to the farmyard. Bouncing the football as we went, we'd make for the swings, the slide and the see-saw. But wedding or funeral, early afternoon or late, we never entered the churchyard. The lych-gate was as far as we'd go. You could see those cracked chest tombs from there. 'Summat ought to be done about them, and all,' I heard Mum say once. 'Not right for a young bride to see *death things* on the happiest day of her life.' And I crassly laughed: not that my Dad did, or the girls, or Sally.

The girls, my Dad and my Mum were supporting me when it came to burying Sally. Oh, but she was still such a young woman, and I was inconsolable. After the girls had gone back to their homes with their husbands, and while my Mum cleared up in the house after the funeral reception, my Dad accompanied me down Church Lane and back to the churchyard. I wanted to see and to photograph the labels on the wreaths and bouquets. I wanted to stand beside the grave a while, but not on my own.

'She never wanted to come here,' I said to him. 'To this village, I mean. Our house.'

'Ah,' he said, 'I know she dain't. But you has to tek what life brings.'

'She's not far from where you once said I'd get popped in.'

'You can get popped in with her, your time comes.'

He meant well, saying this. Just for once, I didn't mind him seeing me cry. We clasped each other, the only time. He cried, too. He'd always been very fond of Sally.

He knelt down and took a handful of the new-turned earth and patted it down where Sally's headstone would be placed. It couldn't have been easy for him, what with his arthritic hip. 'You've done all as is right and proper, son,' he said. 'Earth to earth. You'll have your memories. Come on home, now.'

When my Dad's time came, I was surprised when we read in his Will that he wanted to be cremated. I drove my Mum up to the midlands, some weeks later, and we had a short service in his family's village church before depositing his ashes in the red earth of my granddad's grave. It left my hands stained.

These events took place some years ago. For a while, I hated this house; I almost came to the point of selling up and going to live abroad. But then the grandchildren came along, who had never known Sally, and I was happy to see them playing in the garden. I was able to feel a love for the place similar to that which I'd felt for it when we first moved here.

And so things might well have continued until my time would have come: plodding along, visiting my Mum, tending Sally's grave, having my daughters bring their families of a Saturday midday for lunch, walking round the village, the recreation ground, the farmyard, the churchyard – had it not been that a new lady came into my life.

People tell me that if I remarry, the lady and I will never find happiness unless we move elsewhere. This is still *Sally's house*, they say. But I like it here. I do. When you get to my age, you don't want to shift all your stuff. If I did remarry, when I died I suppose I wouldn't be popped in the plot I bought for Sally and me. 'Till death us do part' means that.

Last night was Christmas Eve. For the first time, I sat in what was once the girls' bedroom, maudlin, awash with whisky, waiting to see whether the White Lady would appear. I rather fancied she might, and I imagined how she'd look. Like Sally, of course. If she did walk, I wasn't awake to see her. In the linen cupboard, just a quarter of an inch through the party wall, through which she was supposed to pass, is the chest in which I've kept Sally's wedding dress. I've promised my grandchildren that, when they come later today, they shall open the mysterious chest. They'll want to see their Mums, one after the other, wearing the white dress and the billowing veil – perhaps briefly outside in the garden, where the snow's flying like confetti. I'm not ready yet to talk about my new lady. Hers, too, will become a presence in the house – in time. I'm staring at ordinary walls in an ordinary room. I don't know what to think, let alone what to do.

CHRISTMAS PEARS

After he's fetched home the Christmas pears, he'll have his favourite time alone: that hour of Christmas Eve while the daylight fails before the dusk, while the dusk then fails before full dark. He'll leave the fruit in its box on the kitchen table; and someone (but who?) will discover the pears after coming home and finding him not there. He must remember to leave the lid half-open, revealing four full rows of unblemished fruit nestling in royal blue tissue paper; Comice, Conference, William – pears whose very names can be savoured in the mouth and on the lips. The scent of pears in a house in midwinter bodes well for those that live there.

Maybe he'll use his solitary hour walking the shore where, whatever the state of the tide, the year will be at its lowest ebb: tamarisks ragged above high-water line and snagged with wisps of sea-weed; delicate, summer-painted beach-huts newly slammed and splintered by gales; the flung spray and fistfuls of weather spitefully stinging his face like nettles or insults.

Or perhaps he'll drive north, up to the Downs to a clearing from which he can look down and identify his house – if its lights should come on before he leaves, that is. It's where he goes when he needs to sort things out in his mind and

197

get things into proportion. Up there, where England's loveli-est beech trees were felled by a great hurricane, you can survey the city with, at its exact centre, the glimmering stained glass of its cathedral. (The congregation will have entered during the candid light of afternoon; they will have seen fat candles lit; before long they will emerge into the vastness of a nightfall no number of blazing, department-store windows can begin to illumine. It is the hour of the Nine Lessons and Carols, that hour containing a moment when unbelievers want to believe.)

Up in the clearing, where the elegant, silver-barked beeches had used to stand – where, during that terrible year, he also shivered with a grief still raw from his unaccountable loss – he fancied he could hear, carried in the wind off the sea, the strains of exultant and echoing voices: voices of choir and people; the voices, too, of the immense brass pipes of the organ making everything and everyone in the cathedral shudder. He thought – with optimism, and joy, and hope, and vastly inexpressible love – of all his still-living loved ones down there, somewhere below where he was.

And suddenly his solitude was no longer a blessing or a balm. No light had come on in his house; in the air was no sound of singing. He had the acutest sense of being his own ghost revisiting familiar ground, some future Christmas Eve. He imagined how somebody (who?) would enter a kitchen where no box of fruit was wrapped in royal blue tissue-paper; who would sniff and say, half-aloud, 'I can smell the scent of pears, there has always been love in this house.'

Which is why he hurried home through the rain. And found them all returned, his family, in the blinding light of the kitchen, the juice of his gift of pears glistening on their chins.